The Seventh Stranger

The Seventh Stranger

Michael Raff

Edited and formatted by Jenny Margotta,
    editorjennymargotta@mail.com

Cover photo courtesy of dreamstime
Back cover and interior photo courtesy of canstock photo

Printed in the United States of America

Published by:

Other Books by Michael Raff

Special: A True Story
Seven: Tales of Terror
Scare Tactics
Shreds
Skeleton Man
Stalkers
Shadowland
Something Different

May be purchased on line at:

amazon.com
mraffbooks.com
and
Nevermoreenterprises.com

ACKNOWLEDGMENTS

I would like to thank my good friend, fellow author, and accomplished editor of all my anthologies and novels, Jenny Margotta. Without her keen eye, industrious red ink, and flair for the most subtle of blunders, my work would not be the same. Also, I would like to thank the remaining members of my critique group, aptly named "The Dark Side": Freddi Gold and Roberta Smith. They have endured through thick and thin with me, and between them they have made countless catches and helpful suggestions. And once again, I would like to thank the High Desert Branch of the California Writers Club for providing me, along with my fellow members, a vast array of useful information by way of guest speakers, writing and marketing insights, and other helpful information.

Finally, there is my wife, Joyce, who has read everything I have ever written . . . well, not the stuff I wrote when I was a kid, but everything else. Without her support and putting up with my endless hours at the computer, this book would not have been possible.

For my cousins:

Gee Caulder
and
JoAnne Hiley

"Invisible things are the only realities"

—Edgar Allan Poe

The Mansion

Dennis and Danny Jensen pulled their bikes onto the shoulder of old Highway 113, nowadays nothing more than a beat-up stretch of deteriorating asphalt. They hadn't seen a single car or pedestrian for nearly half an hour. Both boys rode Schwinn bicycles: thirteen-year-old Dennis rode a 26-inch Racer, 10 speed, and nine-year-old Danny's was a 24-inch Racer, 3 speed. Their father, the founder and owner of Jensen Construction Company, had purchased the bikes used but in good condition. The boys parked between what was left of a rotting tree stump and an old, nearly bare weeping willow tree. The climate in Santa Domingo had always been dry and windy, whether winter or summer, and practically no vegetation could be seen in this barren area.

Danny, who'd just celebrated his birthday, felt tired and thirsty, and his legs had grown sore during the final mile of their journey. They'd been riding an hour and seven minutes exactly. He knew that because he'd kept an eye on the new Timex watch his Uncle Harry and Aunt Karen had given him. Both the bike and watch had become his prized possessions, unlike his big brother Dennis, who favored a coin collection he had inherited from Grandpa Jensen seven months before. The much-beloved patriarch of their entire family had suffered a long illness from an insidious stomach cancer. His death had saddened Danny in particular. Other than their cat, Argyle, who had died of old age the previous July, it was his first encounter with mortality.

The boys stepped off their bikes and planted their kickstands on the rocky ground. Danny kept a wary eye on the sun, which was rapidly headed west. They'd left home much too late, in his opinion, and if they didn't start back soon, their return ride would mostly be in the dark. Although he would never admit it, especially to his big brother, Danny didn't like being out after sunset. Too many bad things happened to kids at night, according to the five o'clock news. Just last month a little girl had disappeared in Bush Creek while on a camping trip with her family. Coyotes or some other savage beast, like maybe a wolf, bear, or even a mountain lion, had probably dragged her off.

Danny swallowed down a suddenly dry throat and forced himself to think about the present situation. Along with his brother, he peered at what stood before them: the Breckinridge Mansion, a place that had to be older than Mother Goose herself. A three-story monstrosity that, surprisingly enough, wasn't in horrible condition, just a few dozen or so shingles missing, and in need of a paint job. The windows were boarded up, but a lower one had been stripped of its planks and the glass broken. Additionally, piles of dirt and all kinds of trash littered the enormous porch that appeared to wrap itself around the mansion. To Danny's overactive imagination, the house resembled a giant with its squarish head jutting from the ground, the gable windows on the second floor its eyes, and the front door its nose.

Danny wiped the sweat from his forehead and, quite unexpectedly, shuddered. Although not well-known outside the city, the mansion was said to be haunted, a claim Dennis constantly badgered him about, *especially* at bedtime. In his most sinister voice, he told stories about kids like Danny going into the mansion and never coming out. Danny had even had a nightmare about the place, something that seemed to encourage Dennis's taunting. Big Brother was a mean, lowdown, disgusting bully, not to mention dimwitted.

Danny had been putting up with his brother's behavior all his life—it was time to teach him a lesson. That was why Danny had decided to go along with the smart-aleck's scheme and ride their bikes all the way out here. But, now, just looking at the mansion made Danny's knees want to knock until they were broken.

The nine-year-old took an anxious breath and turned to his brother. It seemed like a good idea to reason with him. "I-I don't know about this place, Dennis. Going inside . . . seems really stupid." He shrugged. "And maybe not even safe. Something could fall down from the ceiling and hit me on the head. Then what would you do? It's a long way home."

Big Brother smirked and placed his hands on his hips. "Don't tell me you're gonna chicken out after coming *all* this way."

Danny winced. "It's getting late. If we don't start heading back pretty soon, we'll miss dinner. Mom and Dad are gonna be mad. You don't want us to get grounded, do ya?"

Dennis kicked a rock with the tip of his shoe. "Excuses, excuses. You got more of them than Chef Boyardee's got noodles." He reached into his pocket and pulled out his silver dollar. Not just *any* silver dollar but a 1921 Morgan, 90 percent silver, with a grade of "fine" to boot. The year 1921 was a great year for Morgans; it was the last year they were issued. Both boys knew this because Grandpa Jensen had gone on and on about his coins. When he died of cancer, he left Dennis half the collection, and their older sister, Stephanie, the other half. A disappointed Danny was stuck with a 500-dollar government bond that would mature in ten years. He felt hurt and cheated. Ten years was a heck of a long time. His brother, a brownnose if there ever was one, had all the luck.

With his eyes locked on his younger brother, Dennis flipped the coin and caught it, a blatant gesture of temptation, like sticking a carrot in front of a donkey. "Did you forget about this gorgeous beauty, chicken liver? Twenty minutes in a harmless mansion and it's *yours,* buddy boy."

It was weird how, according to Dennis, the mansion had been demoted from a death trap to a harmless building once the bet was made.

"Otherwise, you owe me ten bucks and have to kiss Benny's butthole."

Danny cringed. It would be bad enough losing ten dollars—a total of five whole weeks of allowances—but smooching their Bull Terrier's behind, with his chronic gas problem, terrified the life out of him. How did someone like himself with plenty of brains get into this mess?

"Well, what's it gonna be? My most *valuable* silver dollar or having to cough up ten bucks and enjoying a *hot date* with Benny?"

"How come *you're* not coming in?" Danny fired back. He figured he had a darn good point there and wanted to pat himself on the back. "Staying out here where it's safe makes *you* the chicken."

"That isn't a part of the deal," snapped Dennis. "That would make it too easy. You had at least one nightmare about this place that I know about, and by going in and facing your fears, you won't have any more. Plus, you'll have my coin." He grinned like a crocodile creeping in for the kill.

Danny groaned. His brother was full of horse crap. "You're a real creep, you know that?"

Big Brother laughed. "That's what you get for being so clueless."

"I don't trust you." Danny held out his palm. "Hand it over first, then I go inside."

Dennis raised an eyebrow. "Okay, okay. I admit, sometimes, I haven't been very cool to you, but you know me, right? You know I've kept my word each and every day of your pathetic life." He dropped the coin into his shirt pocket and flashed his most snooty grin. "The coin will be right here waiting for you, I promise. In twenty minutes it'll be yours."

Danny gulped, his saliva tasting like castor oil. Feeling depressed, he turned toward the mansion. It seemed to be staring at him like it was going to gobble him up for a tasty snack. Then he focused on Benny's butthole versus the silver dollar. He took a determined breath and clenched his fists. "Okay, that's it, smartass. This time I'm gonna *win*. Just be ready to hand it over. If you don't, I'm going to the folks and spill my guts out!"

Dennis was never someone *not* to have the last word. "No

problem. I'll be waiting for ya," he shot back. "Good luck. Can't say it's been a pleasure knowing ya." He smiled one of his more cockier grins. "Just kidding. You'll be fine."

Danny ignored his brother. He concentrated on the front door as he approached the porch. No Trespassing signs were nailed to two of the wooden posts, as if that were necessary. The mansion gave him a thorough case of the creeps. If only the next twenty minutes were already over. He grabbed the right-hand railing and climbed the steps to the porch. Nearly every floorboard creaked. He inched toward the door and tried turning the handle. *Locked. Oh, well. Too bad. Time to go home.*

"What did you expect, bonehead?" his brother hollered from the edge of the property. "For the door to be *unlocked*? Go through the broken window, but watch out for glass."

Danny crept to his right and checked his watch: 3:44 exactly. A pile of lumber stood in front of the busted opening. It was obvious the window had been boarded up and someone had ripped the wood down and broken the glass. A lot of trouble for a bunch of nothing. Guess he wasn't the first person to trespass. He checked the window frame for glass and swatted away a handful of fragments. It was dirtier than Benny's doghouse! He wiped his hand on his pants, stepped on top of the wood pile, and reluctantly eased through the window.

***

Inside, everything seemed to change. The air grew musty, colder, and the surroundings much darker. Danny glanced from left to right. He was standing in a bare living room with a large wooden stairway to the left. Except for a stone fireplace, and a lot of dust, dirt, and cobwebs, the room was empty. The outside of the mansion looked a lot better than the inside, he concluded. Nearly every wall in the room had holes, a few of them nearly a foot wide, with lots of rubble on the floor. He frowned and wondered just how old this place was. Did Davy Crockett sleep here? Probably not, but maybe Big Foot had.

Danny checked his watch: 3:45 exactly. Only nineteen minutes to go. He took what was meant to be a calming breath and ended up sneezing. His nose had become irritated, with a bunch of snot building up inside. His eyes were watering like leaky pipes. Not only did the mansion smell bad, but he was allergic to all the filthy dust, and he might start sneezing until his head exploded—or he puked his guts out.

Approaching the fireplace, Danny decided he didn't like what he saw. He'd been too busy being creeped out and hadn't spotted something even more creepy. To the right and left of the fireplace were statues of some kind of winged monsters, both about five feet tall. They flaunted curled snouts, pointed ears, twisted horns, sharp claws, and even sharper teeth. He didn't know what they were, but they looked familiar, and he thought he'd seen some of them in books or magazines. There was no question about the monsters—they were like something out of the TV show *Tales from the Darkside*. Who would want creatures like them in their living room? The Addams Family? Good thing they were only statues.

Danny sniffled and spat on the fireplace's hearth. His nose felt a little better, but he was going to have to breathe though his mouth. Plus he was having trouble taking his eyes off the monsters. *Calm down. No way can they hurt me. Just wait until I get out of here. I gonna kick Dennis right between the legs.*

Feeling better, Danny glanced at his watch: eighteen minutes to go. He turned toward the staircase. He would look around a little more and then hole up down here—but nowhere near the fireplace. He had no interest in going upstairs. It wasn't like he was scared. Well, maybe a little, but not too much. He just wanted to make sure everything nearby was okay and then wait out his time. The silver dollar was going to be his. Boy, would that ever teach that slob brother of his a lesson.

As Danny approached the entryway just opposite the staircase, he heard something behind him. A strange sound, one that he had never heard before and couldn't begin to describe. Taking an anxious breath, he clenched his fists and turned around.

The living room appeared to be even darker, but as before, there was still plenty of dirt, dust, and cobwebs, not to mention the holes in the walls. He began to exhale. If nothing was there, then what had made that strange sound? He peered at the fireplace. As if he'd just been drenched with ice water, his blood turned cold. The monsters had freed themselves from the walls. Turning their heads toward him, they licked their chops and stared at him with starving eyes.

Monsters

A single, obnoxious fly kept landing on Dennis's left ear, trying to get inside. The thirteen-year-old cursed and swatted at it, smacking his ear. He winced and opened his eyes. All he could see was the darkening sky. He recalled sitting down, leaning against the tree stump and, after that, must have dozed off. That was weird. He'd never done that before.

Yawning, Dennis glanced at his watch and jumped to his feet. "Four-fifty! What the hell?" He looked around for his little brother. Evidently, Danny was still in the mansion, and it been for over an *hour*. Grumbling, Dennis tripped over a tree root, stumbled into his brother's bike, and knocked it over. Where was the douchebag? And what the hell did he think he was doing? Trying to scare him? Trying to get Big Brother to come inside? He had a good mind to get on his bike and leave the little toad behind.

Dennis peered west and discovered the sun had set behind the mountain pass. It was twilight and getting darker by the minute. He felt the wind kicking up against his face. Typical for Santa Domingo this time of day. Although his little brother didn't want anyone to know, he was gutless about the dark—*very* gutless—so it seemed unlikely he would be pulling some stupid disappearing stunt.

Suddenly, Dennis had a bad feeling, a rarity that bewildered him. He took a deep breath and cleared his throat. "Hey, numb nuts, where are you?" he hollered, straining his lungs. "You were supposed to come out a long time ago."

He waited for a response, doing his best to be patient, which was never easy when it came to his little brother. The seconds ticked by. He counted to sixty. Still, there was no response. He raised his voice and nearly ruptured his vocal cords. "Danny, you'd better get out here on the double . . . or I'm gonna *kick* your *ass*!"

There was nothing like a good threat to get the twirp motivated. Again, Dennis waited, expecting to see his kid brother climbing from the broken window or rushing through the door, probably all dusty and dirty right down to his shoes. Maybe even with a wet spot running down his leg. But again, nothing. He'd shouted so loudly that a deaf person could have heard him all the way in downtown Santa Domingo. The bad feeling grew and he didn't like it one bit. He didn't want to go into the mansion but what else could he do? Maybe the little idiot fell down some stairs or something. As it was, they were going to be late and not home in time for dinner. Man, oh man, their folks were going to kill them. He'd better get going and find the little turkey.

Dennis hurried toward the front porch. For the first time since waking up, he recalled the mansion was rumored to be haunted. He flinched and shoved the memory out of his head. He didn't believe in ghosts—mostly because he'd never seen one. He felt ghosts were stories made up to frighten little kids—like his brother—but he had to admit anything was possible. He caught himself cringing. The last thing he should be thinking about was such scary stuff.

Stepping onto the porch, Dennis rushed to the wood pile, climbed on top of it, then stuck his head through the window. "Hey, you jerk! Where are you?"

Again, he waited and, again, there was no answer. He found the silence irritating and frustrating, but most of all, unnerving. He became more and more aware of his heart, of how it thumped harder by the minute. He couldn't believe it, but a cold, fiendish shiver ran down his spine. If anything happened to the little creep, Mom and Dad would never forgive him. And worst of all he would never forgive *himself*, something he didn't like to admit it, but it was true nevertheless.

Dennis hurried through the window and paused to let his eyes adjust. As dark as it was getting outside, it was even darker in the mansion. Damn! Why didn't he bring a flashlight? It would certainly come in handy.

Built into the far wall was a very old and enormous fireplace made out of rocks, probably from around this area. It was strange, but on either side of the fireplace, both walls were damaged as if something had been yanked from them, and there was a lot of rubble on the floor directly below and some more rubble on the hearth.

Dennis shook his head. He was being distracted. He'd better find Danny. The long ride home suddenly felt intimidating, and they were going to be grounded until they were broken-down old geezers.

"Hey, Danny, you better come out, or so help me—" His voice echoed in the bare room. Of course, there was no response. Exasperation crept through him. He was going to have to search the place. If the kid was hurt, that was one thing, but if he was goofing around, playing some dumb game, then how many years would he get for murdering the baboon?

Dennis took a last look at the fireplace and moved into the entryway. He could hear the wind outside whistling through the broken window. A huge, wooden, spiral staircase, also covered with dust and cobwebs, towered over him. He knew his brother. Danny would never go up the stairway. He wasn't *that* stupid. He would probably look around for a little while, then hole up someplace downstairs and wait out the twenty minutes.

Grumbling under his breath, Dennis moved across the entryway to the next room, stepping through a pair of open doors. "Danny, where are you? This ain't funny! So help me, I'm gonna clobber ya!"

The room was gigantic, with a high ceiling, built-in wall

shelves and a chandelier all but obscured by cobwebs. A considerable amount of junk littered the floor, mostly dirt, old newspapers, and chunks of plaster from the damaged walls. He groaned. His anxiety escalated. *No Danny here. Better move on. Why doesn't he answer?*

The bad feeling grew a little more. How weird. He'd never been worried about his brother before. He had always thought he hated the little creep.

Dennis made his way down a long corridor. Stained and peeling wallpaper lined the hallway. Encroaching darkness hampered his progress. A doorway emerged on the left and he peered into the ruins of a bathroom. All he could make out was a filthy sink and counter, plus a cracked and stained mirror in which he could barely see his reflection. Just a black silhouette with no facial details. Like a ghost itself, only darker. His mind raced. His head throbbed. He fought off confusion and discouragement but couldn't overcome his mounting guilt. What the hell was he thinking, making Danny come inside? Was this place actually haunted? Did some type of perverted ghost kidnap his brother? How in the world was that possible? How could any of this craziness be happening?

Turning, Dennis returned to the hallway and inched toward the kitchen. His anxiety reached its zenith and his heart pounded. He couldn't believe his reactions. He'd always thought the little idiot was like a bowling ball tied around his neck. He sighed and rolled his eyes. All that had changed in the last few minutes. Now, all a sudden, he felt guilt-ridden and was stressing over the kid.

Dennis entered the kitchen through a lopsided swinging door, its hinges barely attached to the door jamb. A partially boarded window filtered in a scant amount of light. More litter. More cobwebs. The room was a disaster. It was as if the floor were made of dirt instead of linoleum. Or was it ceramic? He couldn't tell. Bits of broken glass were scattered all over, sparkling in the fading light. It felt as he'd descended into the pit of hell itself. He discovered a back door and a dilapidated cast iron stove that looked to be from another century. He halted, held his breath, and listened for the longest moment of his life.

A barely perceptible noise emerged, what could only be described as a muffled yelling. Dennis turned toward the source—the battered door of what had to be the pantry. The noise was followed by a loud and desperate banging from the inside. His heart nearly shot out of his mouth. *That's gotta be Danny!*

Dennis hurried to the pantry and flung the door open. It took a moment for his eyes to adjust. Danny was sprawled across the floor, his hands tied behind his back, his ankles bound together. His mouth had been stuffed with something he couldn't make out. He wore no shoes, no socks. Apparently, he'd been kicking the door with his bare feet.

"For crying out loud! How did this happen? Where's your shoes and socks?" Dennis dropped to his knees and pulled two objects out of the kid's mouth. He'd just found his brother's socks. "What the hell? Who did this to you?"

At first all Danny could do was gasp for air. In the dim light Dennis could make out his brother's eyes, which were riddled with terror, and how his body had started trembling.

"M-monsters!" Danny cried, his voice panicked and piercing. "With scary *red* eyes like blood. They *attacked* me, tied me up! Monsters from the fireplace!"

Dennis shook his head and untied his brother's hands. He couldn't believe it. The kid had been tied up with his own shoelaces. First the socks, then the laces. His own belongings had been used against him. Now he was talking screwy. "There aren't any monsters. Maybe you're crazy or hallucinating. Somebody tied you up. Maybe some weirdos in costumes or something. You're always getting into trouble. I can't take you anywhere."

"I'm not crazy! And I'm not hallucinating," Danny hollered. "Ya gotta believe me."

Together they untied his ankles. "You're worse than crazy," murmured Dennis. "You're *batshit* crazy. It had to be somebody, an actual *person*. There's no such things as monsters."

Danny shot to his feet. "Yeah, well tell *them* that. Now, let's get out of here."

A fluttering sound intervened, a flutter like a very large bird with huge wings would make. A shadow crossed the light filtering through the partially boarded window, followed by a second shadow about the same size.

"They're back," Danny shouted, slamming the door shut, the echo deafening in the small space. "It's *them*. They're after me. And now they're after you, too."

Dennis felt his mouth drop open. He wanted to deny the whole situation. His brother was suffering from shock, or hallucinations, or something like that. Then his doubts came to a grinding halt and what felt like an icy hand gripped his heart. He *heard* the fluttering. Like a huge bird or bat. And he *saw* shadows—moving shadows—just beyond the pantry door. He'd rather eat five gallons of asparagus than admit it, but as far-fetched as it sounded, he suddenly believed his brother. *Something was out there.* At least two of them. Maybe not monsters, but something that had gagged and tied up the kid.

"What are we gonna do?" Danny clutched his brother's arm.

Dennis peered about the pantry, hoping to find an object he could use as a weapon, like a broom or a frying pan. All but blind, he felt along the four shelves from top to bottom. Because the darkness kept slowing him down, it took much longer than it should have. He swore under his breath. Nothing but dust and dirt clung to his hands . . . and maybe a few mouse turds, as well. His frustration grew. Dusting off his hands, he patted his brother's shoulder. "Okay, calm down. We're gonna have to make a break for it."

"The front door's too far away," Danny whimpered. "They're quick. They'll *catch* us."

"There's a door in the kitchen. It's only about forty feet away. If we run, we'll be all right. You're gonna need your shoes. Where are they?"

"I don't know. They took them while they were dragging me around. It was horrible. I-I thought I was gonna *die*!"

"Shh, not so loud." Dennis knew his brother. Although he couldn't see his face, by the tone and volume of his voice, he knew the kid was terrified. "No sweat. We'll get out of here. Stay calm. Find your socks. There's glass on the kitchen floor and you're gonna need your socks for protection."

Danny searched the pantry and Dennis placed his ear against the door. He heard another flutter, then another. Whatever they were, they were in the kitchen, waiting for them to come out.

"Got 'em," Danny croaked. He dropped to the floor and slipped his socks on. "Okay, let's go." His voice was loud enough to wake someone like good, old King Tut.

"Knock it off, damn it. If you want to make it out of here, we have to wait. And for Pete sake . . . *lower* your voice." Dennis listened for what felt like an eternity. He heard a flutter, then another. What in hell were they doing out there? Changing positions? Getting ready to attack? Then all grew quiet. He swore he could hear Danny's Timex, ticking off each and every grueling second. His heart took a steep dive. What had he done? Because of his constant picking on his brother, they were now in trouble. He'd always told himself he pushed the kid around to make him tougher so he could defend himself against the bullies at school. He sighed. Maybe he was just kidding himself. His little bet with Danny had totally backfired—on both of them.

Dennis felt a single drop of sweat trickle down his face. He shoved back his anxiety. He had to concentrate on the situation. It had been quiet for at least a minute now. If they didn't act soon, it might be too late. Taking a deep breath, he whispered, "Get ready."

He eased the door open a few inches and listened some more. The silence had grown nerve-wracking, but he thought it was a good sign—or at least a *decent* one. He peeked out for a fraction of a second but couldn't see anything. Leaning toward Danny, he counted to three, his voice hushed and determined. Then, grabbing his brother by the arm, he hollered, "Go!"

Both boys flew from the panty and raced toward the kitchen door. Dennis pushed his brother ahead of him. Halfway there, he tripped and landed on his hands and knees but still managed to strike his forehead on the floor. Intense pain engulfed him. Dirt had flown into his eyes. Wiping them, he raised himself to his knees.

Danny reached the door, unlocked it, and flung it open. Dennis could distinguish a black sky brightened by an array of stars. "Come on," Danny hollered. "Get up!"

Dennis struggled to his feet and staggered to the door. Danny rushed into the night just as his older brother started to catch up. As Dennis ran up to the door, he turned and peered back into the kitchen. The murky outline of a large, winged creature, nearly the size of a man, had perched itself on the counter. A second winged creature crouched just behind the pantry door. Dennis gasped out loud. His heart pounded. Burning a blood-red color just as Danny had described, the creature's eyes glared at him with undeniable viciousness.

Wishing he had never looked back, Dennis flinched and slammed the door shut.

Danny grabbed his brother's arm. "Come on. Hurry up. Let's go!"

They ran to the front of the mansion as if chased by the devil himself. The ground proved treacherous. They stumbled and nearly fell. By the time they reached their bikes, Danny was limping. If only they'd had enough time to find his shoes.

As they jumped onto their bikes, a horrific sensation raced through Dennis. He placed his hand on his shirt pocket, and he thought he would die of grief. "My silver dollar! It's gone. I must have lost it when I fell."

A large, nearly full moon gave them enough illumination for Dennis to see Danny's reaction. It was as if he were dumbfounded by his brother's stupidity. "I don't care anymore," Danny screamed. "Let's go!"

Dennis gritted his teeth and again swore under his breath. Although he'd risk losing the coin to Danny, it was still his most prized possession. He considered going back for it then recalled the creatures' blood-red eyes. They'd be waiting for him. Heading back would be suicidal. Like diving into a wood chipper. Speechless, Dennis could only nod. They hurried home, peddling as fast as they could.

Their efforts were wasted. Their parents grounded them for two whole weeks then piled on more punishment: no television, no allowance, an eight o'clock bedtime, and no dessert after dinner. A near-death sentence if there ever was one. Life had turned into a cruel and unfair disaster.

Dennis didn't want any more trouble, so they lied about the creatures, claiming they rode all the way to the Breckinridge Mansion on a dare from Eddie Ratcliff, a snotty, know-it-all from school. On their way home, however, Danny had argued to spill the beans about the monsters. He thought telling the truth would probably get them off easy. But knowing their parents wouldn't believe any stories about monsters, Big Brother convinced him that the lie was the best way to go.

For the second time in his life—the first while they were trapped inside the mansion—Dennis felt remorseful. He gave his brother two silver dollars, their combined value equal to the Morgan. But he never forgot his 1921 silver dollar. It remained a prickly thorn in his side for years to come. Losing it, and his actions prior to entering the mansion, had taught him a lesson in humility. He dreamed about retrieving the coin but couldn't bring himself to return to that awful place.

*** *

There were other consequences beside the punishments. Consequences a lot worse than the ones their parents had given them. A week or so after the mansion disaster, Dennis heard Danny crying in his sleep. They slept in separate beds in the same bedroom, Danny on the right under the window, Dennis on the left against the wall.

"No. No. No!" Danny yelled, waking his brother from a dream about taking Deborah Ann Miller to the movies. "Go away, go away!"

Dennis sat up, rubbed his eyes, and peered at Danny. The kid was sitting up, wide awake and looking at their open closet. Dennis sighed and glanced over. A pair of blood-red eyes stared back.

Danny's nightmares continued on and off for months. Thankfully, never again did either of them wake up to be confronted by a pair of blood-red eyes.

***

Twenty years later, after Dennis had turned thirty-three, something extraordinary happened. An event well beyond his wildest dreams. A lot of people believe there are no such things as monsters, heaven, hell, God, the devil, or ghosts. But not Dennis Jenson.

The Morgan

Dennis pulled his Chevy Silverado onto the gravel driveway. Both his front doors displayed "Jenson's Construction" signs. He turned off the ignition and stepped on the emergency brake.

Both Dennis and Danny had started working for their father while they were still teenagers. They began as gophers running errands, worked their way up to measuring and sawing two-by-fours, painting, installing drywall, and so on, learning the business from the ground up. When Dad retired due to his much-abused spine, the brothers took over. That was six years ago.

Everything went smoothly and business flourished, but Danny kept missing work due to his longstanding problem—drugs: cocaine, meth, hash, you name it. Dennis would have fired him if it weren't for the fact that they were partners. So older brother had stepped up, filled in for Danny, and worked overtime.

A sense of gloom crept through Dennis as he recalled the tragedy that had changed everything three years ago. Danny had been killed in a head-on collision—his own fault—the autopsy results verifying that his cocaine level had been nearly off the charts. Little brother had started his habit at sixteen. He had never recovered from that time so many years before at the mansion. How could a little more than an hour cause such trauma to a kid like Danny? How could it affect him for the rest of his life? One bizarre disaster causing a domino effect that would eventually kill him.

Dennis sighed and peered out the driver's window at the Breckinridge Mansion, the source of his brother's terror, and, as far as he was concerned, Danny's addiction as well. Life wasn't only filled with coincidences; it was loaded with ugliness and tragedy.

Having completed his restoration project, the mansion's exterior appeared quite normal, or more accurately, majestic, even beautiful, as such older mansions often were. The interior looked better yet, every nook and cranny restored. But that was on the surface. To Dennis the mansion had *never* felt normal.

The previous year, when he discovered that the Breckinridge Mansion was the job he'd been bidding on, it was as if he'd been struck by a semi. At first he took a pass. It was a no-brainer: he, his brother, and the mansion had a history, a rather brief and frightening one that invoked memories best left forgotten. But First National Bank of California had remained persistent. None of Dennis's competitors would touch the place for less than 200 grand. The mansion's dismal condition required a major overhaul.

Dennis finally agreed to inspect the place, along with John Randall and Hazel Johnson, the bank reps. Despite the years of neglect, Dennis knew he could restore the site for less than $200,000. He decided that business, not to mention a profit of roughly fifty grand, won the day. Still, he was plagued by ambivalence and doubt when he had placed his bid.

Now, almost a year later, here he was, about to conduct his final walk-through before the bank handled theirs and then—finally—the project would be signed off by the city of Santa Domingo. Once the final installment had been paid, it was adios Breckinridge Mansion and he would never cross paths with it again.

It had been a long project for him and his crew of six. They handled everything: electricity, plumbing, roofing, the works. Of course, Dennis pitched in and made sure they were finished every day before sunset. Maybe that helped. Despite his fears and dread, little had happened out of the ordinary. His crew mentioned a few strange sounds, bumps, creaks, and such. Leonard Jackson swore he spotted a young girl out of the corner of his eye but when he turned around she had disappeared. Carlos Fonseca swore he felt a sudden chill, as if someone had stepped through him. And Dick Stewart claimed he had heard voices from the upstairs but when he investigated no one was there.

Dennis himself heard what sounded like the crying of a little girl from the back yard. When he looked out the kitchen window, there was no little girl, but one of the seats on the swing set was actively swinging before coming to an abrupt halt.

On the last day at the site, when the final coat of paint had been completed, Dennis breathed a sigh of relief. He'd made the right decision and was enjoying his most profitable year ever.

Naturally, he took an interest in the so-called "monsters" that bordered the fireplace. The very ones that had chased his brother, tied him up, then stalked both of them. The culprits weren't *exactly* monsters, but *gargoyles*, fictional creatures that supposedly protect churches and other buildings. Danny had been too young at the time to know what they were. Months later, when Dennis discovered one in a magazine, he brought it to Danny's attention. With anxiety seeping into his eyes, his brother confirmed their identity.

Regret tore through Dennis like a meat cleaver. His only brother, who had suffered from night terrors and drug addiction, was already three years in his grave. If only he'd treated him better when they were younger. He was quite certain that he'd been successful after the mansion disaster. What had happened brought them together as never before. The ordeal they'd shared had put an end to their rivalry, pettiness, and jealousies and put them on equal terms. For that, he would always be grateful.

Dennis sighed, grabbed his clipboard, and climbed out of the truck. Enough reminiscing. Time to get to work. He made his way to the front porch, typed in the combination on the lockbox, and removed the key. He felt relieved. This was his last time in the mansion, but strangely enough, he felt a little sorry, as well. His crew had done a remarkable job restoring a rundown heap into an object of beauty and elegance. He was proud of their work, and the so-called supernatural incidents had turned out to be harmless. No one would lose any sleep over such minor episodes. His only regret: not taking his triphammer to those butt-ugly gargoyles.

Dennis closed the front door and headed to the staircase. He would inspect everything upstairs first, including the lights, plumbing, carpeting, and the ceramic and wooden flooring. Just as he expected, the entire upstairs checked out perfectly.

Descending the staircase, Dennis couldn't help but smile, although it was a half-hearted one at best. Not one stair squeaked. Quite the accomplishment, considering that, when they began, the entire thing was about to collapse. He made his way through his favorite room—what he thought would make a terrific office or library, surveying the walls, electrical outlets, floor, ceiling, and built-in bookcases.

As he stepped into the living room, Dennis forced back a shudder. Turning the lights on and off, he scrutinized the walls, ceiling, floor, and finally, the fireplace. He paused mere inches in front of the hearth and forced himself to look at the two "monsters." Complete with horns, sharp teeth, claws, and bat-like wings, their eyes remained vacant—so unlike that night when they were blood-red and full of viciousness. After all these years, he wondered how it was possible that something made of stone could come alive and terrorize two kids for the rest of their lives.

Twenty years. It seemed like a lifetime ago. Screw them. Taking an angry breath, he flashed his best shit-eating grin and gave the gargoyles the middle finger.

Dennis entered the downstairs bathroom and recalled what a disaster it had been when they first started. He checked the lights, flushed the toilet, and turned the faucet on and off. One more room to go and it would be so long to the Breckinridge Mansion. A minor event for sure, but one he'd been looking forward to.

As Dennis entered the kitchen, however, it felt as if an alien was nibbling at his belly, trying to make its way out. Such craziness happened every time he came into this room. If only he could erase those memories, banish them forever. He inspected the swinging door, tested the lights, then the faucet, the garbage disposal, and the stove. He opened the door and entered the pantry—where he and Danny had found themselves trapped. He sighed. Do people share the same hallucination? He supposed not, but if they did, that would certainly make life simpler. What an ugly secret to keep locked away in the darkest regions of your mind for twenty years. He shook his head. He missed his brother. Danny was right up there with his wife, Ellen, and his daughter, Rebecca. All of them first-rate. Checking off the pantry on his clipboard, Dennis returned to the kitchen. Time to head out.

As he approached the hallway, he heard a metallic sound striking one of the counters. A chill ran through his body. Turning, he spotted a coin rolling on its edge across the counter next to the sink. He watched as it plunged onto the floor without so much as breaking its stride. It rolled across the kitchen floor toward him, struck the toe of his boot and, spinning in a hypnotic fashion, fell onto its side.

Dennis froze in uncertainty, took a skittish breath and peered at the coin. His heartbeat increased. His breath caught in his throat. The coin was a 1921 Morgan silver dollar. *His silver dollar,* looking as impressive as the day he'd lost it.

For an instant, the room spun. He closed his eyes and waited. All those months working in the mansion and nothing like this had ever happened. He opened his eyes and peered at his feet, hoping the coin had disappeared. But it remained, sparkling like a gem in the afternoon sun. His mind reeled with endless questions. Why had this happened? Was some unseen entity—grateful for restoring the mansion to its original luster—offering him some type of peace token? His suspicions escalated. That type of thinking could prove dangerous.

Perhaps the coin was bait. A trap for the adult version of the older brother. He swallowed and, taking his time, studied the Morgan. Its beauty and value enticed him.

Dennis swallowed and took a long, calming breath. Outside, the wind rattled the window over the sink. Why was he hesitating? It was *his* silver dollar. There shouldn't be a problem with him taking it. Overruling the alien in his belly, he picked up the coin with a jittery hand. Clenching his teeth, he placed it in the palm of his hand. With the face of Lady Liberty on the front, and the eagle on the back, it remained in what appeared to be "fine" condition. It felt solid and tangible. Something *real*. How was any of that possible?

"Thank you," Dennis murmured under his breath. It all seemed bizarre, utterly impossible. But the mysterious force within the mansion—the same force that he'd long ago concluded controlled the gargoyles and emotionally scarred two kids—had just attempted to make amens. At least, that was how it appeared to him. He felt grateful and, even more so, relieved. All those years of horrible memories would never be wiped clean. But the gesture was better than nothing.

An intense burning stung Dennis' hand. He dropped the dollar and grabbed his palm. The coin bounced twice, rolled a few feet, then landed Lady Liberty side up. What followed all but paralyzed him, hurling him back to that night twenty years before when all hell had broken loose.

Lady Liberty came alive, squirming about as if she were in unbearable agony. She burst into two halves as dozens of maggots swarmed from her body. Dennis inched backwards, wishing to God he was having a nightmare. He wanted to scream until his lungs burst. He wanted to tear his eyes out. *What the hell? This can't be happening.*

Once the maggots stopped emerging, they squirmed across the floor then burst into flames. A chorus of miniscule screams echoed through the kitchen. As Dennis watched, the coin melted, every centimeter bubbling like lava. Tears flowed from his eyes. Before he could take another breath, his beautiful Morgan transmuted into a smoldering stain on the newly tiled floor.

Dennis rushed from the kitchen, locked the mansion's front door, and hurried to his truck. He couldn't get the keys out of his pants pocket fast enough. All the while, he heard laughter—low, maniacal, laughter—bellowing from the living room window. A face appeared behind the glass. But it wasn't a face, not in the least. It was something else; it was a human skull, half covered with rotting flesh, and flaunting bulging eyes that burned a bright blood-red.

The McKays

For over fifty minutes, Jake and Lindsey McKay had been gasping nonstop. The Breckinridge Mansion was magnificent, right down to its finest detail. Including the attic, it featured three stories with over 5,500 square feet, five spacious bedrooms, a winding staircase, lush carpeting, and solid hardwood flooring throughout. There was even a basement—almost unheard of in California—covering the entire length of the house. Outside, the massive front porch with its sturdy wooden railings circled both sides of the mansion. To the right of the front door was an old-fashioned, hanging swing, large enough for three adults. Shutters adorned every window. The most striking detail was the gables that looked down at the front yard from two of the guest bedrooms, a gothic and unusual feature straight out of the nineteenth century.

Not every aspect of the property was picture perfect. The back yard included a battered and rusty children's swing set. At the north side of the house stood a detached garage in obviously rough condition and, beyond that, an acre of neglected apple trees.

Located on old Highway 113, the house was two miles distant

from Interstate 88. Custom built prior to the Civil War, the Breckinridge Mansion was a true rarity, everything their real estate broker had claimed and more.

Jake, Lindsey, and Mrs. Hampton, the real estate woman, paused in front of the fireplace, a massive structure that dominated the living room. Featuring tannish-colored river rock from its sprawling hearth to its oak mantel, the sight of it left Lindsey speechless. Then there were the gargoyles bordering its sides. She found the sculptures disquieting—like refugees from a chamber of horrors—and the only feature inside the mansion she disliked. What were the builders thinking? Why not sentry soldiers, lighthouses, lions, or anything else other than a pair of hideous beasts? Just like the mansion, however, the fireplace was a one of a kind, both beautiful and majestic—minus the gargoyles. After they'd settled in, if she had anything to say about it, the nasty creatures would be on their way out. Perhaps they could relocate them to some obscure Catholic church in Europe—but only at the *Vatican's* expense.

Forty-one-year-old Jake limped in his usual manner, caused by a knee wound he never talked about, a reminder from his Vietnam days. It made his life harder on a daily basis, especially today, as he traveled up and down the staircase. To Lindsey's delight, however, he managed it with a grin plastered across his face. During the walk-through, he stroked his short, well-groomed beard when he wasn't adjusting his glasses—positive signs of his enthusiasm. Clearing his throat, he turned to the stout, middle-aged real estate woman. "Outstanding," he proclaimed. "But I doubt if we can afford it. Not on the salaries of a nurse and a high school teacher."

Already tapping on her calculator, Mrs. Hampton flashed one of her most charming smiles. "You're in for a surprise, Mr. McKay." Peering at the couple, her eyes sparkled with boundless enthusiasm and confidence. "How does two ninety-nine sound?"

Lindsey stepped forward, her eyes wide, her mouth agape. "T-two-ninety-nine, that's all? Are you kidding?" She bit down on her bottom lip. There had to be a catch.

"Well, that's *rock bottom*. It includes the five acres, which still need work. However, as you've seen, the interior has been *completely* restored." She smiled once again. "When I say that two ninety-nine's remarkable, I'm *not* just whistling Dixie."

Peering from the chandelier to the fireplace, then back to Mrs. Hampton, Jake's eyebrows nearly danced off his forehead. Lindsey couldn't wipe the grin from her face. First, the low selling price and, now, Jake at a loss for words. How wonderfully incredible. But her mind kept returning to the same doubt: there had to be a catch.

"With your sixty thousand dollars down, the payment should be around seventeen hundred a month. A little high I know, considering your income, but with money coming in from the apple orchard, and renting the spare bedrooms as bed-and-breakfast hideaways, you could *easily* afford seventeen hundred."

Jake slid his hands into his pockets and started swaying on his heels. Lindsey could tell he wanted the mansion, possibly more than she did, right down to the glass doorknobs. Suddenly, Jake's forehead wrinkled. "Mrs. Hampton, this place has got to be worth more. How can the owner afford to sell it so . . . cheaply? There's gotta be a catch."

Lindsey nodded. As usual, her husband had beaten her to the punch.

The real estate woman slipped the calculator into her blazer pocket. "Well, for one thing, this house doesn't have an owner. The last one died years ago. The mortgage belongs to First National Bank of California, and they're losing money every month while it sits on the market. They spent a fortune restoring the place, and they're eager to cut their losses."

Sighing, Mrs. Hampton glanced around the living room. Lindsey noticed how she avoided looking at the gargoyles. No wonder, they probably gave her nightmares. The agent's confident manner vanished and the sparkle in her ever-expressive eyes disappeared. "I'll be honest with you, Mr. McKay. There's always something about an older home that . . . well . . . spoils a good sale."

Lindsey glanced at her husband. His forehead had grown *especially* wrinkled. "Continue, Mrs. Hampton," he urged. "We appreciate your honesty."

The woman began fidgeting and Lindsey braced herself.

"According to folks familiar with the mansion—" She paused, swallowed, and took an anxious breath. "Well . . . *supposedly* . . . this lovely home is haunted."

Jake cracked a smile that would make even the most professional gambler nervous. Lindsey shook her head and her heart plunged. She knew her husband. Spontaneity could very well be his middle name, but when it came to buying a home, however, he was the epitome of caution. "Haunted, like in *ghosts*?"

Mrs. Hampton raised a hand. "Well, *supposedly*, but I've seen *nothing* wrong with this beautiful home, ghosts or otherwise. I'd be willing to wager my last dollar on it."

Lindsey scrutinized her husband with an analytical eye. Under that John Deere cap, the wheels of selective reasoning were burning circuits. Taking his hands out of his pockets, he turned, peered at the gargoyle to the left of the fireplace, then turned back to the realtor. "We're talking about a haunted, nineteenth-century mansion. Am I right?"

The woman forced an anxious smile and nodded.

Jake chuckled and motioned at his ears. "For a minute there, I thought I'd better get my hearing checked."

"I don't believe in such hogwash myself," Mrs. Hampton continued but not before blushing three shades of scarlet. "But these rumors persist. According to the stories, there are at least *six* ghosts who inhabit this mansion."

Again adjusting his glasses, Jake nodded. "Six ghosts. I see. That must be some kind of record. Maybe we should call Guinness."

Appearing as pale as a ghost herself, Mrs. Hampton seemed to be coming out of her skin. Lindsey felt sorry for her. Everything had been going so well until now, so well for all three of them. Yet she felt herself the *real* loser. The real estate agent may have lost a commission, but Lindsey McKay was losing a marvelous, one-of-a-kind home. What would have been her dream come true since she was a teenager.

"Yes, six ghosts, including the original owner, Colonel Sedgwick Breckinridge, a Civil War veteran, the man the house was named after." Again, the agent sighed then rolled her eyes. "The construction crew reported some strange noises and perhaps *one* sighting during nearly a year of restoration." She raised her index finger. "But when it comes to such stories, you should take them with a grain of salt. There's nothing *unusual* about hearing noises in a home this old. And working in such a huge mansion can play tricks on a person's mind, especially after hearing the rumors." She paused and took a heavy breath. "I thought you should know about this . . . *before* making up your minds."

Lindsey sighed, trying to fight off her discouragement. "Are these ghosts dangerous in any way?"

"Oh, heavens no!" Mrs. Hampton gushed, waving her hand. "Absolutely not. I've *never* heard of a ghost hurting anyone in this mansion or anyplace elsewhere. Even if they do exist, I'm quite sure ghosts are harmless."

Again, Lindsey scrutinized her husband. Behind those thick glasses, his eyes had remained locked on Mrs. Hampton. Tugging at his earlobe, he nodded, then turned toward Lindsey. "Honey," he began, his voice breathy, his forehead relaxing. "I don't know about you, but I think we should jump on this. We can make a fortune renting out rooms in a *haunted* house. Besides, it's a *fantastic* deal. Especially compared to where we're living now with all the noise, traffic, and pollution."

Lindsey found herself struck speechless once again, but this time in a happy manner. Rallying herself, she hugged her husband and nodded.

Jake turned to the real estate woman and shook her hand, all but ripping the poor lady's arm out its socket. "Mrs. Hampton, you've got yourself a deal." Grinning as if he'd just won the lottery, he peered back and forth between Lindsey and the agent. "When can we move in?"

***

Three months later

Rushing out of the mansion, Jake hiked up his pants and headed toward his Tundra parked in their gravel driveway. He, Lindsey, and their six-year-old daughter, Heidi, had just moved into the mansion two days before. Jake's right boot struck an embedded rock and he struggled to recover his balance. His bum knee had been giving him lots of trouble since they had moved in. Lugging around furniture and boxes was always hard on him. Vicodin and icepacks had become a part of his nightly routine. Lindsey had been after him to have his knee replaced, but the surgery would put him out of commission for quite some time. The idea of not being able to do what he wanted, when he wanted, never sat well with him.

So far no bogeymen were rattling their chains and keeping them awake at night. Not that he minded, but maybe Mrs. Hampton had been taking those rumors much too seriously. He and Lindsey were still unpacking, and they both had tons of work to do before starting their new jobs the following week. Today's project was to drive to town and pick up a load of PVC pipes at Ace Hardware. His friend Rick was driving in from Woodland Hills to help Jake install the sprinkler system, a two-man job, considering the rocky terrain. Although a lush front lawn seemed unrealistic, especially in this type of climate, not to mention the drought conditions, he would settle for a few more trees, a handful of rose bushes, and a healthy flowerbed.

Jake retrieved his keys from his pants pocket, climbed into the Tundra's cab, and cranked the ignition. He checked for traffic before backing out. How strange. A white Silverado was parked on the shoulder about a hundred feet from the mansion. A guy sat behind the steering wheel, and there was a business sign on the driver's side door. Jake tried but couldn't make out the lettering.

Lindsey had often badgered Jake about his pessimistic nature. And yeah, he could admit that a time or two it had boarded paranoia. In this case, however, a reasonable dose of pessimism seemed like a good idea. Was the guy stalking them, or had his truck broken down? If it had broken down, wouldn't he have propped up the hood and be phoning AAA? Or maybe knocking on their door for some help?

Jake stopped the Tundra at the end of the driveway. He'd better talk to the guy and find out. A little voice in his ear butted in, a soft, mellow type of voice that, unsurprisingly, sounded like Lindsey's. *Are you being too suspicious? Always looking for creepy crawlers under rocks?* Jake groaned and kicked the pesky voice out of his head. *Not this time.* He wasn't about to leave Lindsey and Heidi alone with a stranger parked nearby.

Grumbling, Jake pulled onto the shoulder in front of the Silverado. He peered in the rearview mirror and watched as the guy climbed out of his truck. He looked to be in his early to mid-thirties, wore work boots, jeans, a white T-shirt, and a blue cap with a logo he also couldn't make out. The guy was on the skinny side and looked as if he hadn't shaved for a while. Was he a Charlie Manson in disguise? Or did he want his battery jumped? The guy was headed his way, so he obviously wanted to talk. Jake shook his head. There were too many crackpots these days in Santa Domingo, but at least most of them dwelled in the downtown area. Jake climbed out of the Tundra.

The guy casually closed in. His hands were stuffed into his pockets and he was smiling in what appeared to be an uncomfortable manner. "Guess you're wondering what I want," he murmured as he approached.

Jake braced himself. "Yeah, guess you could say that."

"I'm Dennis Jensen. My crew and I restored your house." He offered his hand and Jake wanted to inch away. The guy was sweating through his cap, which he now could read. Jensen's Construction, probably local, and the name sounded familiar. To his surprise, he smelled beer on the guy's breath, not a good sign since it was only ten in the morning.

Jake accepted the handshake, although reluctantly. Dennis had a weak grip and his palm felt calloused and clammy. "I'm Jake McKay. What can I do for you?"

Dennis returned his hands to his pockets and peered at the mansion. "This isn't going to be easy for me to say, Mr. McKay, but I thought I should warn you. There's something . . . terribly wrong with your home."

Jake folded his arms across his chest. "You mean because it's supposed to be haunted? That's what we've been told, but so far no ghosts have popped out of the woodwork. We've only been here a few days, though, and we're still unpacking."

Dennis looked at him as if he were a babbling lunatic. His eyes grew wary and he appeared to be on the verge of some type of meltdown. "It's more than haunted." There was an edgy tremor in his voice and in the matter of an instant, the expression in his eyes had gone from wary to frantic. "I don't know how to explain it, but you better reconsider living here. It's not safe. You and your family are in danger."

Jake took a guarded breath, unfolded his arms, and adjusted his glasses. "What do you mean? The real estate woman said the construction crew experienced a few *minor* episodes. Nothing to worry about." He straightened his shoulders and took another breath. "Did something else happen to you? Something I don't know about?"

Inching away, Dennis peered back and forth between the mansion and Jake, his expression a mixture of fear and loathing. "If I told you, you would think I'm crazy, and I don't want to go there. My crew restored that house, and I'm sorry we did." He paused and Jake could clearly tell the man was struggling to continue. "There's something in there that's evil and dangerous. Just pack up your family and *leave*. I thought I should warn you, that's all. If I were you, I'd think long and hard about it."

Dennis rushed off to his truck, looking over his shoulder at the mansion several times as he did so. Jake considered going after him but decided not to. The Breckinridge Mansion was practically legendary in the area, as he had later found out from Mrs. Hampton. No doubt the subject of a lot of loose talk and speculation. But then again, maybe the guy was a former mental patient who had suffered a relapse.

Dennis climbed into his Silverado, slammed the door, and turned on the ignition. Hitting the gas, he raced past Jake toward the interstate, dirt billowing in the air. He never looked his way.

The Domino Effect

On the way back to his motel room, Dennis stopped at King's Liquor, which he'd been frequenting much too often according to his estranged wife, Ellen. *This will be my last six pack*, he promised himself. *When it's gone, I'm quitting for good.* Ever since the catastrophe at the Breckinridge Mansion six months before, his drinking had skyrocketed. But getting shit-faced, falling-down, slobbering drunk was his way of blocking out memories he desperately wanted to forget. Unbearable and god-awful memories that, as far as he was concerned, only happened to insane people or clueless victims in horror movies.

Climbing into his Silverado, he glanced around for any police cruisers, opened a can of Budweiser, and downed a sizable gulp. He felt some guilt about not waiting until he was back at the motel but he fought it off. He wiped his mouth, started the truck, and pulled away. He had wanted to attend Rebecca's birthday party the previous Saturday night. The little munchkin had just turned seven, but the ever-protective Ellen wouldn't let him inside their house. "Not until you sober up," she had demanded, her voice emphatic.

"You're treating me like some kind of alcoholic," he had fired back. "An alcoholic who's a *worthless loser*."

Ellen had placed her hands on her hips. She could be plenty stubborn when she wanted to. "I never said you were a loser. I just don't want you drinking around our daughter. All you do is stumble around and act like an idiot. Try to get past your pride for a second, then you'll understand my position." Tears had welled in her eyes. "My father was a total drunk, and because my mom didn't know how to handle the situation, I ended up hating him."

Dennis had stood on their front porch, holding a bouquet of carnations for her—his way of saying sorry—a teddy bear for Rebecca, and a six pack of Bud for himself. "Take me back, Ellen. I know I'm not the best husband, but I can change. I just need you to be patient with me."

"I'll take you back when you straighten out. Spend some time with your parents, maybe they can help. Then go see a therapist, and better yet, join AA. I don't know what's eating you, because you keep everything locked up inside." She stopped to wipe a stream of tears from her face. "But you can't change on your own. You need help. You're ruining everything in your life—your business, our marriage, and your relationship with Rebecca. Now go. Everyone's on their way for the party. Don't ruin this for your daughter."

What could he have said to that? He had to leave. If only he could get himself together. Six months ago everything had been different: he had a happy family life and a thriving business. Then there was that last day at the Breckinridge Mansion. The memories haunted him on a daily basis. History had a way of repeating itself. He was experiencing the same downhill slide as his kid brother. Only Danny had chosen drugs to block out his torment.

Dennis wanted to scream but couldn't. Shoving Ellen, Rebecca, and his problems out of his head, he pulled into the parking lot of the Stater Brothers grocery store and put the Silverado in park. Gasping for air, he rested his head on the steering wheel. He'd better leave Ellen and Rebecca alone until he pulled himself together. He was making everything worse by bothering them. He knew his wife, and at this rate a restraining order just may be coming his way.

Lifting his head from the steering wheel, Dennis finished the can of beer. It wasn't just the memories of the gargoyles that gnawed at his sanity. Nor was it the melting silver dollar and the maggots that had burst from it. He had seen all kinds of things these last six months. Horrible things that kept him awake at night. Glimpses of shadows and movements out of the corners of his eyes. Glimpses he could never quite distinguish. Something from the mansion had followed him home, followed him to work, and followed him everywhere else, watching his every move. Now that he had warned Jake McKay that he was in danger, the situation would only get worse.

***

Dennis stood at the entrance of the viewing room. Confusion crept through him. He couldn't imagine why he would return to the mortuary that had buried his brother. Sensing trouble, he peered around. He was alone, but everything seemed out of proportion. The walls were colorless and slanted. The ceiling looked too low. The casket stood against the far wall. Its color wasn't right. It had turned from silver to blood-red. The longer he looked at it the more the size changed. One moment it was too small for an adult then, within seconds, it grew larger. On the casket's side facing him there were deep, ragged claw marks that only a large predator could make. The single wreath of flowers at the foot of the casket had withered and died. The ticking from an unseen clock accelerated into a relentless pounding. He stood frozen, holding his throbbing head, his confusion escalating. *What is this? What am I doing here? I buried Danny a long time ago. This can't be right.*

An icy hand squeezed the back of his neck. A voice he didn't know hissed, "You're here because I want you here."

Dennis whirled around, searching, only to find he was still alone. Ambivalence struck. He didn't want to go into the room, but knew he had to. He owed that much and more to his only brother. He had told the funeral director he wanted a *closed* casket, but now, this time around, the lid was open. He couldn't see Danny's lifeless remains from the doorway. When he had identified the body at the morgue, his brother's face had been mutilated beyond recognition. It was as if the windshield fragments had gouged out every square inch of flesh from the kid's face. Even after the morticians had worked him over, an open casket remained out of the question.

Dennis inched his way inside the viewing room. Shouldn't the air smell like flowers? Instead, it smelled stale and musty. A cold, cruel shudder sashayed up his spine. Another odor emerged—the exact kind of odor as when he had found a dead deer in the woods while his family was on a camping trip. One thing about the scent of death, once you caught wind of it, you never forgot it. *Okay, quit stalling. Just get this over with.*

Clenching his fists, Dennis crept down the aisle between the rows of chairs. His heart pounded. This wasn't making sense. Danny had died a long time ago. He approached the casket and braced himself. His eyes widened. He couldn't believe it. Danny looked perfectly normal: unscarred, lifelike, and as incredible as it sounded—boyish. The gauntness from years of drug abuse had been vanquished. The boy he'd known so many years ago had returned. The morticians had done a wonderful job. A butt-kicking, miraculous job, right up there with Moses parting the Red Sea.

Dennis leaned forward and wiped away tears. His heart ached with a passion he had never known. His little brother looked so peaceful, as if he were sleeping. Dennis fought the urge to pat his sibling's shoulder and whisper, "Hey, Danny, wake up. Time to hit the road." He leaned closer, his emotions reeling. "I'm sorry, little brother. I tried making it up to you. I honestly tried. I was a shit until—"

Danny's eyes shot open, staring, but without a sign of life. Dennis jumped back, his heart threatening to explode. It took a moment for him to realize he wasn't in danger. Calming himself, he inched forward until he stood over Danny again. How unacceptable. His brother's eyes shouldn't be open. They should be closed as before. The morticians should have taken care of such a simple, everyday detail.

Reaching down, Dennis closed his brother's eyes. His hands shook. His mouth dried out. He quivered and gazed at Danny. So much better. He was back to being at rest. Peaceful and happy.

Danny's eyes popped open, this time staring at the ceiling with hate and vindictiveness. A look that clearly demanded justice. *Why all that hate? All that . . . rage?*

Dennis summoned what remained of his courage and forced himself to again close his brother's eyes. Why was this happening? The whole thing was ludicrous. He kept running his hand over Danny's eyes, but his efforts were wasted. They would not stay closed. Dennis shuddered. More bad news. The kid's eyes had grown out of proportion. So large that they bulged from their sockets.

The room turned frigid. The stench of death intensified. Dennis watched as the muscles in Danny's face began moving—moving as if he were coming alive, moving as if he were trying to speak. Slowly, silently, his little brother turned his head toward him. Stunned, Dennis stood paralyzed.

"You killed me!" Danny roared. "You sent me into the mansion." Blood dripped from his eyes. The gaping wounds from the accident returned. "*You're* responsible. *You* caused my death. *You're* the one who deserved to die. Not me."

Dennis backed away. He didn't want to look anymore. He had never wanted to look in the first place.

Danny sprang up into a sitting position like a demonic jack-in-the-box. The blood that seeped from his bulging eyes turned black as coal. "You bastard. You took my life." His voice changed from one of anger to one of outrage. "You'll die soon enough . . . a death beyond hideous, beyond anything you can ever imagine . . . and then I'll be avenged."

***

Dennis shot up in bed, his heart racing, his body covered in sweat. It took some time to realize he was only dreaming. The same dream he'd had for months, but more detailed and vivid this time.

Wide awake, he peered at his watch. It was nearly eight o'clock. He shook his head. God damn it, it was eight o'clock at *night*. He scanned the room, fighting through his stupor. His heart sank. He was in the same old filthy dump, the Desert View Motel, the uncontested toilet of Santa Domingo. He cringed and cursed. If only Norman Bates would show up and put him out of his misery. His stomach grumbled. He hadn't eaten anything substantial in days. His throat felt as if it had been lined with cotton and his bladder threatened to rupture. He sighed and wiped his eyes. His liver wasn't the only organ being ravaged by alcohol.

Stumbling out of bed, he made his way to the bathroom. Greeting him, a cockroach jumped off the counter and scrambled across the linoleum. Dennis started to laugh but ended up coughing. "Morning, Conrad," he muttered, creeping toward the commode. "How did you like those cookie crumbs I left?"

Urinating, then flushing the toilet, he approached the sink and peered into the mirror. The image before him stared back in horror. He hardly recognized himself. His hair was tangled and matted, his eyes puffy, and the stubble on his face not only made him appear shabby but sinister. He'd seen homeless people who looked more hygienic.

"You screwed up," declared the image in the mirror. "If this ain't rock bottom . . . then, buddy, you're in some pretty *deep* shit." Once again, it was *his* image tormenting him—but this time, it was *Danny's* voice.

Returning to bed, Dennis flopped onto the mattress. The frame creaked and his head spun. He didn't want to be at the motel, but he'd worn out his welcome at his parents' house. Besides, he wanted solitude, enough time to think things over. Now that he was determined to quit drinking, he was looking forward to moving back with his wife and daughter. But how much damage had he done? Rebecca was only seven-years-old. Kids that age tended to forgive. But then there was Ellen. She could hold a grudge until doomsday, and who could blame her? He inhaled a calming breath. She had promised to take him back, and as long as he'd known her, she had never broken her word.

But there were other issues to contend with. Issues even *more* pressing. He had to prepare himself. Memories of the mansion were hard enough to deal with. Seeing things out of the corners of his eyes, and sensing that something from that godforsaken mansion was after him, those types of issues were *beyond* pressing. *Pull yourself together, damn it. Ghosts don't go after people like that.*

Again, he chuckled. Back when he was thirteen, he didn't even believe in ghosts.

Dennis sighed and eased off the bed. He would drive to the café downtown and treat himself to a meal. That would be a good start. Then he would figure things out.

Returning to the bathroom, Dennis glanced around. Same old dump. The sink was stained, the mirror was streaked, and there was mold growing on the ceiling above the shower. Maybe he should skip showering for now. Tomorrow was Saturday and he could sleep in. He would make the best of the situation. From now on, everything would be uphill.

Dennis rinsed his face with cold water and reached for the hand towel. He opened his eyes and again looked in the mirror. This time a skull stared back—a skull with blood-red eyes and rotted flesh trickling down its face.

Stumbling back, Dennis wiped his eyes and looked again. Only his own reflection stared back. The skull's disappearance did nothing to comfort him. Rushing into the bedroom, he threw on his clothes, scooped up his keys, and hurried out. His heart pounded. His thoughts had grown more confused and scattered than ever. He climbed into the Silverado and started it. He wasn't going to the café. His plans had changed. He jammed the truck into reverse and hit the gas. Beer cans rolled around on the floor of the truck. When he nearly slammed into a passing car, the driver screeched to a halt and blasted his horn.

Screw this. I don't know why this is happening, but I'm not crazy. Ellen's going to have to change her mind. I'll tell her everything about the mansion, but first, I'm going to talk to that McKay guy, or whatever his name was. Warn him one last time. If he doesn't listen, then it's his own damn fault.

The world was suddenly unlivable, his life on the brink of destruction. He floored the gas pedal. The sound of squealing tires breached the cab. Sweat poured down his face. Strange, but how could he be sweating when he was shivering as if he were in the dead of winter?

Once again, Dennis spotted movement out of the corner of his eye. This time the image didn't disappear. Something about the size of a dragonfly stared at him from the passenger's air vent. Dennis nearly drove off the road. Whatever it was, it was difficult to make out. Clutching the steering wheel while holding his breath, he eased up on the gas. Bracing himself, he focused his attention on the vent. A creature flaunting horns and wings peered at him. It remained motionless, staring at him with its head tilted to the left.

God, no! It's one those things from the fireplace.

Another gargoyle poked its head out, this time from the driver's air vent. Since it was so close, Dennis could distinguish its long claws, sharp teeth, and blood-red eyes.

Everything happened at an accelerated speed. Dennis nearly lost control of his vehicle and it seemed to be fighting him every foot of the way. It jumped a curb and sideswiped a tree. He bounced from his seat and rammed into the driver's door. He was terrified. He couldn't keep his eyes on both the gargoyles and the road at the same time. Somehow, Dennis managed to swerve back onto the street as more horror struck: he realized he had forgotten to buckle his seatbelt. Wrestling with the strap, he slammed down on the brake. His blood ran cold. The brakes weren't holding. What in God's name was happening? He wasn't crazy and wasn't drunk.

Gasping for air, he doubled his effort with the seatbelt but something yanked it back. The truck barreled through a red light. More tires screeched. Another horn blasted. His Silverado barely missed a SUV. His mind had become trapped in a maelstrom, scattered thoughts flashing like strobe lights until, suddenly, he recalled what his brother had said to him from the casket.

You'll die soon enough . . .

Tears ran down his face. No matter what he did, the steering wheel possessed a mind of its own. When he glanced in the rearview mirror, his heart almost ruptured. With its red eyes bulging and its face oozing decaying flesh, the skull from the mansion stared at him with fiendish intensity. Its mouth covered half its face; its teeth were rotted and distorted. Its laughter rampaged through the cab—an evil cackle that brought to mind endless torture and death.

Dennis tried but the steering wheel wouldn't budge. The skull had taken control of it, the brakes, and the gas. The Silverado sailed over another curb, barely missing two teenagers and a woman pushing a baby stroller. Consumed by fear and panic, Dennis covered his eyes and braced himself. The truck crashed headlong into a streetlight at sixty miles an hour.

Dennis's last thoughts were of his brother—of how he had died in a similar way.

Into the Fire

After giving Rick Buchanan a complete tour of their new home, Jake led his friend of over twenty-four years to the front porch. Shaded by an enormous roof, the structure was made from the finest grade of cedar. Sitting on the porch swing, they sipped their Coronas and peered at the magnificent view of the mountain pass.

"Well, what do you think, Uncle Rick?" Jake asked, stroking his beard.

Rick, a screenwriter for Morse Studios in Burbank, chuckled. Tall, lanky, and in his late-thirties, he brushed a lock of blond hair from his eyes. He enjoyed their little game of calling each other "Uncle," an inside joke they had started years ago. "Well, *Uncle* Jake, you'll get no argument from me. It's an incredible bargain." He paused and glanced around at the barren terrain. Other than the scraggly weeping willow tree that stood near the street, and the apple orchard at the rear of the property, there was nothing but rocks and dead shrubs. "It's a great house at a great price, but it's in the middle of nowhere. What makes you think people will want to rent rooms out here? There's nothing to see, nothing to do."

Using the side of his boot, Jake nudged away a beetle. It reacted by sprouting wings and taking flight. "People don't need anything to do. It's a *romantic* hideaway. Besides, we're basically on the way to Vegas. The only complication is—"

Staring past the red and white Sold sign he had asked Mrs. Hampton to get rid of, he admired the view of the mountain pass. He was trying to find a way to tell Rick about the supernatural aspect of their home—without sounding crazy.

"And?" Rick prompted.

"And this house is . . . well . . . it's different in that it's supposed to be—"

Suddenly, the screen door swung open. Six-year-old Heidi came flying out of the house, making her usual grand entrance. She'd been taking a nap and hadn't been able to greet their visitor when he arrived. "Hi, Rick!" she cried. She jumped into his lap and planted a kiss on his cheek.

Rick gave her a hug. "How's my girl?"

"Great, I'm glad you're here!"

Rick laughed and hugged her some more. "Me too." He peered at Jake, his eyes reflecting a touch of envy. "Boy, one of these days, I hope to have a little girl just like yours."

Jake smirked and sipped his beer. "You'll just have to slow down on cranking out those screenplays of yours and take some time to find a compatible woman."

Heidi tapped Rick on the arm. "Did you see our new home?"

"Yep, your dad gave me the grand tour."

"But you didn't see *my* room." She peered at her father. "Can I show him, Daddy? Please?"

"Later, sweetheart, Uncle Rick and I want to talk. Besides, there's work to be done." He glanced over at his friend. "As usual, your visit's well-timed."

Rick nodded. "Yeah, well don't work me *too* hard, Uncle Jake. I'm on vacation."

"Installing a sprinkler system in this terrain isn't *hard* work. It's what I call backbreaking." Jake chuckled. "Like being on a chain gang, I would imagine."

Heidi glanced back and forth between them. "Hey, how come you guys keep calling each other uncle?"

Rick put the little girl down. "Well, since we live so far apart, in order to stay close, your dad and I decided we should be related."

Heidi gazed at her father. "Is that true, Daddy?"

Jake laughed. "Close enough. It started when his niece gave him a 'Greatest Uncle' T-shirt. Now, go play. You can visit with Rick later."

With that, Heidi took off, running around to the back of the house toward the swing set, a rusty eye-sore Jake couldn't wait to tear down.

Grinning as if his latest screenplay had just been sold to Steven Spielberg, Rick blurted, "Wish I had that kind of energy."

Jake stood, reached toward the railing, and handed his friend a shovel. "That makes two of us. Speaking of energy, you want to get started?"

"You bet. Just try to keep up with me." Slipping on his sunglasses and a Universal Studios ball cap, Rick asked, "Now what were you saying about your house?"

"My house?"

"Yeah, you know. We were discussing why you bought it. Something about it being different."

Jake took Rick by the arm. "Come on, we're burning daylight. I'll tell you while we're working. I think you're gonna find this stuff interesting."

***

Sitting on a swing and sliding her feet along the ground, Heidi came to a stop. A tad wary of heights, she would only swing so high, especially on this rusty old playset. She was facing the garage, which was to the right of the house. The unrestored building was in need of a paint job and looked like it was ready to fall down. So far she hadn't seen it from the inside nor did she care to.

There was a gravel driveway leading up to the garage—which led to a seldom-traveled road Daddy referred to as a "highway"— that twisted and turned its way to the interstate. Parked in the driveway was Rick's white Chrysler convertible. Behind both the garage and the house, the apple orchard covered almost half the property. To Heidi their land looked humongous. Maybe even bigger than Disneyland.

With all this space, would Daddy *finally* buy her a puppy? She'd wanted one for over a year now. The house they had lived in before had been small and the back yard even smaller. So Daddy had kept putting off looking for a puppy. Heidi felt as if she were jumping out of her skin just thinking about owning a dog she could call her own. The only problem was . . . would she get a Poodle or a Yorkie?

Boredom quickly crept into the six-year-old, and she began wondering if the swing set was safe. It creaked too loudly and the slide looked awfully tall for her liking. Rusty and dirty, as well.

As Heidi looked up at the clouds forming overhead, she heard giggling—a faraway kind of giggling, as if it were coming from a deep well. She turned toward the sound and spotted a girl roughly her own age wearing a frilly, pink party dress. The young stranger made eye contact, giggled again, then turning, ducked behind the garage.

How strange. What was she doing here? Was she lost? Should she tell Daddy? And why would she go behind the garage? To play hide and seek? Maybe she knew she was trespassing and didn't want to get in trouble.

Heidi jumped off the swing, hoping to make a new friend. "Hey, wait for me," she shouted, running toward the back of the garage. She glanced around and then peered at the garage's back wall. There was an abandoned refrigerator standing against it, also covered with rust. She thought it might be the oldest refrigerator in world, maybe even older than Daddy!

Disappointment hung over Heidi. Where could the girl have gone? She gazed at the refrigerator. Could she be inside? It was the only hiding place nearby. Mustering renewed hope, Heidi rushed over and tried opening the door. The stupid thing was stuck. It took a few tries, but it finally opened. Once again, disappointment claimed Heidi. Empty. In fact, it smelled terrible, like it was a graveyard for rats but without any skeletons inside. Just a bunch of brown stains and nothing more.

Closing the door, Heidi turned away. Facing the apple orchard, she continued searching. A short distance away, she discovered a narrow gully. Perhaps the girl had gone into it. Yes, that had to be it.

She was hiding down there where she couldn't be seen. But why would she do that? Heidi rushed over to gully's crest and looked downward. There wasn't a trace of the little girl, just broken glass, weeds, and a crunched-up beer can. Yuck. She hated when Daddy drank beer. It smelled awful.

A question made itself known at the back of Heidi's mind. Where had the girl come from? There weren't any other houses around here, which had been her main complaint about the move. No neighborhood meant no new friends. It was bad enough being an only child. Friends were important. Feeling hot and frustrated, Heidi turned around.

An ominous rattling sound knifed through the air. In front of the six-year-old, not more than four feet away, a coiled snake was ready to strike. Not knowing what else to do, Heidi froze. It had trapped her at the crest of the gully. She had heard a lot about rattlesnakes from Mommy, Daddy, and the *Animal Planet* TV show. Rattlesnakes were poisonous. If it bit her, she would have to go to the hospital . . . and might even *die*. Terrified, her heart raced. If she backed away, she would fall into the gully. If she tried moving around the snake, it would probably strike.

"Mommy! Daddy! Uncle Rick!" she screamed.

Remaining in place, Heidi kept her focus on the creature. It was a long way to the house, but maybe Daddy and Uncle Rick had hear her. She waited, a sickening feeling churning her stomach.

A rock flew from behind Heidi and struck the snake just beneath its head, knocking it from its coiled position. Clearly stunned, the reptile took a while to pull itself together, then it slithered away and disappeared behind a crop of weeds.

Relieved, Heidi turned around, expecting to see the little girl. Instead, a beautiful woman stood on the other side of the gully, smiling and wearing a white nightgown. Once again, Heidi froze. The woman was floating about six inches off the ground, and Heidi could clearly see the apple orchard through her. Before the six-year-old could utter a word, the woman drifted behind one of the trees—and did not reappear on the other side.

Confusion overwhelmed Heidi. The tree was too skinny to hide behind. Taking care to avoid the broken glass, she maneuvered her way down into the gully, and up the other side. Sure enough, there was no one behind the tree. What was going on? She had been able to see through the woman but not the little girl. But then again, she hadn't been able to take a good look at the girl. Things like this had never happened to her before. It was like a dream, but here she was, wide awake.

Glancing about the orchard, Heidi decided to get something to drink. Perhaps she would see these people later. Hopefully, if everything went well, she would get to know the little girl *and* the woman, and then the three of them could become good friends.

***

Lindsey had been working hard all day, emptying boxes, storing dishes, silverware, pots, pans, and other items in her new kitchen. She had enjoyed herself at first. As the day wore on, however, her back started to ache. She grew hot and tired and was looking forward to a nice, long shower. Unfortunately, it was almost dinnertime. Perhaps Jake could send out for a pizza? She then remembered where they were living and chuckled. No self-respecting pizza parlor would ever consider delivering all the way out here in Timbuktu.

Glancing around the room, Lindsey felt satisfied. The kitchen had shaped up nicely. Only six boxes remained. She was about to pour herself a glass of water when she heard the noise again—a most unsettling sound—coming from the master bedroom upstairs. She'd been hearing the noise off and on all afternoon: first a bump, followed by a squeak, then another bump, and another squeak. Jake and Rick were outside, working on the sprinkler system. Heidi had come in for some juice but had returned to the back yard, leaving Lindsey without any explanation for the sound. Previously, it had only lasted a few seconds, but this time it remained persistent. *Bump, squeak. Bump, squeak.* Washing her hands then wiping them on a dish towel, she decided to investigate.

Lindsey passed Jake's grandfather clock in the entryway and approached the centerpiece of their new home, the staircase.

Feeling a surge of pride, she couldn't help but smile. The majestic structure—or perhaps an even better description was *breathtaking* structure—was an image straight out of her most beloved fantasy. Something she'd always dreamed about as a teenager, and unlike most of the wooden floors in her new home, the staircase didn't squeak.

Winding upward from the left side of the entryway, the railings, banisters, and stairs were constructed from the finest oak. As it rose to the second floor, the width of the stairs enlarged from six feet to nearly eight. The front posts of the banisters were five times wider than the spindles, with an Art Deco style of grooves that resembled lightning bolts. Functional bronze lanterns, controlled by a dimmer switch on the adjacent wall, adorned the crests of the front posts. In Lindsey's opinion, their staircase was a one of a kind, a creation from generations before that had been lovingly restored.

A hair shy of being "overly compulsive," as Jake had often claimed, Lindsey paused to scoop up a piece of Styrofoam that must have fallen out of one of the boxes. Gripping the banister, she made her way up. *Such great exercise. If only it wasn't so rough on Jake's knee*, she mused to herself. *At this rate I'll be in better shape than Arnold Schwarzenegger.*

Lindsey reached the second floor and turned left toward the master bedroom. She could still hear the noise—a bump followed by a squeak—but now it was non-stop. Moving down the hallway, she discovered the door to their bedroom was closed. How weird. She remembered leaving it open. She always left the bedroom doors open to allow fresh air into the rooms. Just one of her many habits that Jake considered neurotic.

Lifting her hair and wiping away the perspiration from the back of her neck, Lindsey stepped to the door. As soon as she placed her hand on the glass doorknob, the sound stopped. It didn't matter to her. Noise or no noise, she was going to investigate and put this little mystery to rest.

Suddenly, a feeling of dread swept through her. Mrs. Hampton had claimed that their new home was haunted by at least six ghosts. So far, *au contraire*, Madame Eccentric. Not a single ghost had made an appearance. Lindsey licked her lips and swallowed. Hopefully, there would be a reasonable explanation for the noise—and not some spooky individual.

Holding her breath, she eased the door open. The brass hinges creaked, causing the hair on Lindsey's arms to stand on end. With her eyes wide and her nerves on edge, she entered the room but found nothing unusual . . . except for the bed. She had made it before breakfast, tucking in the blankets and bedspread nice and tight, making "hospital corners," as they called them at Saint Mary's Memorial, where she worked. So why were the covers pulled back on Jake's side?

Lindsey remade the bed and ambled out of the room. Her back was feeling somewhat better, and with some aspirin, she could finish the kitchen and start dinner. Jake and Rick would be a while. They loved working together and over the years had formed a type of male competitiveness. They would happily labor until dark like a pair of medieval slaves.

Descending the staircase, Lindsey veered right. She hurried through the dining room and entered the kitchen by way of the swinging door. She had never lived in a home with such an item and didn't care for it. She preferred an open doorway, especially to the kitchen. If someone was coming from the other side, a mishap was bound to happen. Her mind was made up. She would convince Jake to take the door down once they settled in. Next to get the boot would be those butt-ugly gargoyles by the fireplace.

Lindsey rushed through the swinging door then screeched to a halt. A chill rushed through her. *What in God's name?* Dressed in a powder-blue bathrobe and matching bedroom slippers, a woman who appeared to be in her upper eighties gazed at the boxes stacked on the floor. She stood hunched over, her gray hair pulled back, her wrinkled face and hands the color of snow. Whoever she was, she appeared to be a typical elderly woman, except for one disturbing detail—she was utterly transparent and floating six inches above the floor. Both shocked and fascinated, Lindsey stared at her in frozen silence.

The woman must have sensed someone had entered the room.

She whirled around and spotted Lindsey. Her mouth dropped open and her eyes bulged. Rising up, she floated across the room and vanished through the wall over the sink.

An intense lightheadedness overwhelmed Lindsey and she had to grab the kitchen table for support. Once again, Mrs. Hampton came to mind. Until now, Lindsey had assumed that the agent's ghost stories were the products of an overactive imagination. Probably several overactive imaginations. Lindsey enjoyed a Stephen King book every now and then but never entertained belief in anything supernatural. Could her mind be playing tricks on her? Or perhaps Mrs. Hampton's stories had planted a seed of vulnerability? Lindsey frowned. She knew herself better than that. Like it or not, she'd just seen a ghost. Whether she should tell Jake about it, she felt uncertain. Although her husband would gladly charge customers to stay in a "haunted house," Jake was a diehard skeptic and didn't believe in anything he couldn't see or touch.

Stepping to the kitchen sink, Lindsey's knees threatened to buckle. Quite understandable. After all, it wasn't every day she watched a senior citizen float across a room. Turning on the faucet, she closed her eyes and rinsed her face. Instant relief. Her heartbeat began to slow. She started to catch her breath and her lightheadedness dissipated. She felt better and opened her eyes.

Disbelief swept through her. It wasn't water gushing from the tap. It was *blood*, pure and simple. She could see, smell, and taste it on her lips. Not only had she drenched her face with it, but it had splattered across the sink and counter.

Another wave of lightheadedness struck and Lindsey had to shut her eyes. Her stomach took a sharp turn, and thinking she was going to vomit, she bent down over the sink. She gagged but held on.

Suddenly, the blood's distinctive taste ceased. Lindsey opened her eyes. Clear water was again gushing from the faucet. All signs of blood had vanished. Not a trace of it in the sink or on the counter. Although warm and clammy, her face felt dry. *How is that possible? I drenched my face with it . . . and now it's dry?*

Lindsey stepped back and straightened her shoulders. Filling her lungs, she counted to five then exhaled. She repeated the process then relaxed. Enough was enough. She didn't care that the blood had disappeared. She *wasn't* crazy. It had been there; nothing would change her mind. She would take a shower then start dinner. Hopefully, this was just a one-time occurrence and there wouldn't be any blood coming from the showerhead. Now, if she could just get her legs moving—that would be quite the accomplishment.

***

Standing their shovels against an interior garage wall, Jake closed the overhead door and the two men shuffled down the driveway then across the front yard. Hot, tired, and filthy, they collapsed onto the front-porch swing.

"Not bad for a couple of hours' work," Jake boasted while pulling out a pair of cigars from his shirt pocket. "I think it's time for a smoke."

His eyes wide, Rick leaned forward. "Are those what I think they are?"

Jake handed his friend one of the Cubans. "They certainly are, Uncle Rick. A little heaven on earth, compliments of good old Fidel, the scourge of the western hemisphere." The two men lit the cigars and sat back for a moment before Jake continued. "Lindsey doesn't want me polluting the house and I won't smoke around Heidi, so I come out here, especially at dusk, my favorite time."

They faced the mountains and the sprawling pass. Jake rushed into the house and returned with a pair of ice-cold Coronas. Watching the brilliant, scarlet sunset, they drank and puffed on the cigars.

"So, tell me, Uncle Jake," Rick began. "How does it feel to be the owner of a haunted house?"

Jake shrugged. "To tell you the truth, I don't know." He paused and chuckled. "Who knows? Maybe I got conned by a middle-aged hustler in the guise of a real estate agent." He paused, puffed on the cigar, and recalled the look of fear in Dennis Jenson's eyes. He grimaced and dismissed the memory. No sense dwelling on it. "We haven't seen or heard a thing. Just the usual noises from an old house in the middle of a windy desert."

Rick ran a hand through his thick blond hair. "Yeah, but you've only been here for a few days. What if you're wrong? You could be endangering Lindsey and Heidi."

Jake stopped smoking. His face turned colorless. "Endangering? Hell, t-that never occurred to me."

"I'm not a believer in the supernatural," Rick stated. "But I have an extremely bright nephew who swears ghosts are as real as death and taxes."

Jake frowned and rolled the cigar between his thumb and index finger. "You mean your nephew at the college? The zany one?" He noticed that Rick wasn't smoking his cigar and suspected he had accepted it just to be polite.

Rick nodded. "Zany? Yeah, I guess you can say that. Zany, eccentric, probably even more. But he's also a genius, if that's the right word." He broke into a broad grin and turned toward his friend. "My side of the family doesn't get the credit. Julian takes after my brother-in-law's side. Lots of brainpower but not a whole lot of commonsense."

Jake stared at his cigar, his thoughts racing. Glancing at his friend, his face regained its natural color. "We'll be all right, Uncle Rick. Mrs. Hampton, our real estate agent, promised that the ghosts *weren't* dangerous." He eased back into the porch swing, his eyes reflecting utmost confidence. "Even if they do exist, they have no bodies, so it seems unlikely they can hurt anyone."

Rick stared at the pass for a long moment. He shrugged, crushed out the cigar in the ashtray on his lap, and leaned back. His thoughts seemed to be traveling a hundred miles a minute. "I hope so, Uncle Jake. For the sake of your family, I sure hope so."

* * *

Across the front yard, within the shade of the weeping willow tree, something watched the two men. It watched and listened to their every word. As the seconds slipped by, its rage grew. It longed to kill everyone in the mansion, including the little girl. Tear them apart and savor every bloody moment. It fought off its frustration. It was used to getting its way and had *never* been patient. Not for a day, not for an hour, not for a minute. But for now, it had to be. The agony of their deaths would come soon enough. It had grown resourceful and extremely powerful over the years. Every one of those four intruders would pay for this travesty. They would pay with their lives.

The Long Night

"What do you mean you were attacked by a rattlesnake?" Lindsey scolded, leaning over the kitchen table. Heidi put down her fork and lowered her eyes. "This is serious, honey. Why didn't you tell us before?"

Staring at her empty plate with a woeful expression, the six-year-old shrugged. Since she was already in trouble over the snake, she gave up the idea of telling her parents about the little girl and the beautiful woman.

Jake sat at the opposite end of the table, next to Rick, who had just taken a shower and changed his clothes. "Rattlesnake?" Jake murmured, looking so shocked he could barely talk. "Did you say . . . rattlesnake?"

Heidi could almost read her father's mind. As her mother had explained earlier, he'd been so "wrapped up in the house" that he sometimes missed stuff—in this case that rattlers might be hanging out in their back yard.

Lindsey shot an annoyed look at her husband, which seemed to jar him back into the conversation. "Honey, I don't want you to play past the garage . . . or anywhere near the apple orchard," he told his daughter, his voice stern. "From now on, just stay in the yard behind the house, okay? There are too many shrubs and other places where a snake might hide. I'll find a way to keep them off our property so this will never happen again."

Heidi's face turned scarlet. She took a deep breath and asked to be excused. Life wasn't fair. Already bored with playing on the property by herself, this latest restriction only made matters worse. She was starting her new school on Tuesday and, for once, felt happy about it.

***

Lindsey watched her daughter as she left the room. She felt badly about the way she had reacted. Although she hid it well, she'd been on edge ever since the afternoon's confrontations with the ghost and the kitchen faucet. She wanted to tell Jake about it but felt awkward with Rick around. She didn't want one of their oldest and dearest friends thinking she'd lost her mind. Still, Jake needed to know, and she decided to wait until Monday and let the guys enjoy their visit.

***

After Jake and Rick helped clean the kitchen, they settled into a quiet evening of television. Rick, who had been driving all morning, and digging trenches in the afternoon, soon began to nod off. It wasn't long before he excused himself and headed to his room. Lindsey had prepared one of the spare bedrooms, complete with a firm mattress—which he'd already tested—a soft blanket, a cushy pillow, and some privacy. A far better situation than their old house where he had to sleep on their lumpy couch.

In the bedroom, Rick tossed his suitcase on the bed, flipped it open, and pulled out a clean T-shirt and pajama bottoms. He stepped into the bathroom and changed, all the while hearing the wind howling outside. He chuckled. Normally, that would keep him awake, but not tonight. World War III wouldn't keep him awake. He brushed his teeth, staring into the small, beveled mirror above the sink. Even though the room's light was dim for a bathroom, he could still see how puffy his eyes were. It had been a long day, and the weary traveler in the mirror seemed to have aged by a half dozen years. He shook his head, bent down, and rinsed his mouth.

He halted. A chill ran through his body. Always a well-grounded, even-keeled person, for the first time in his thirty-eight years, he sensed he was being watched. He peered into the mirror and through the doorway behind him spotted a dark figure perched on the edge of the bed.

Rick's stomach plunged. Whirling around, he found himself staring at thin air. Zero. Zilch. There was nothing there. Confusion overwhelmed him. He bit down on his bottom lip. All that ghost talk with his friend Jake, and now this.

Keeping a stiff upper lip, Rick inched into the bedroom. Again, the light was too dim for his liking. Too many shadows were created by the faint light from the chandelier. Shadows where that dark figure would be well camouflaged.

Rick sighed and rolled his eyes. The whole thing had happened so quickly that he wasn't sure if he'd actually seen anything. He took a deep breath. The room appeared to be clear of any intruders, ghostly or otherwise, but then he considered the bed. Could what he had seen be hiding under it? He'd better take a look, if for no other reason than to prove that his eyes were indeed deceiving him.

Taking a jittery breath, Rick squatted down by the bed. It took a moment for his eyes to adjust. No dark outline, thank God, for that small favor. Nothing but a smidgin or two of dust. He groaned and stood. A wave of frustration shot through him. Searching under a bed for things that go bump in the night wasn't his idea of a vacation. *Maybe my eyes are playing tricks on me.* He shook his head. *Looks like I was wrong about how nothing would keep me up tonight.*

***

After Lindsey said goodnight, Jake grew restless. He'd been an on-again, off-again insomniac ever since Vietnam. He wouldn't call himself a victim of Post-Traumatic Stress Disorder or even a borderline PTSD case. More like a near miss. He was one of the lucky ones. Over the years, he'd learned how to cope with his past and, at the same time, deal with everyday stresses. His remedy consisted of a regimen of keeping busy, a touch of mind control— he'd read four books on the subject—and plenty of time for relaxation. He would think through whatever issue plagued him, whether past or present, then put it to rest, even if just for the night. When he utilized his remedies *religiously*, he would sleep fine for the most part. He knew he wasn't the most well-adjusted veteran, but he could be disciplined when he needed to.

Stepping out onto the front porch, Jake smoked a cigarette, gazed at the stars, then returned to his office, also known as the computer room. Located across the entryway from the living room and behind a pair of double doors, the enormous room was complete with built-in shelves, a modest fireplace—no gargoyle statues standing guard, thank God for that—and a large picture window facing the mountains. Before the McKays ever moved in, the room had been earmarked for Jake. With his trophy cabinet sitting in a far corner—he played a lot of football and baseball in high school—and his desk beneath the window, only the assembly of his computer equipment remained.

Making as little noise as possible, Jake began his newest project. Before long, the hard drive, keyboard, screen, and printer were up and ready to go. As quiet as the house had been, he kept hearing a squeaking noise in the bedroom above him. Even with the house being fully restored, the upstairs floorboards tended to squeak. At first he thought either Lindsey or Rick was going back and forth to one of the bathrooms. After a while, he realized he was mistaken. The bedroom where the sounds were coming from was vacant. The only other explanation was that Heidi was sleepwalking; there had been at least two episodes in the last three years. He peered at his watch. Midnight exactly. He sighed and decided he'd better check on the noise.

It took Jake longer than usual to reach the staircase because of his bad knee. It had been hurting ever since moving into the mansion. Working his way up the stairs, he turned left. He passed Heidi's and Rick's rooms and made his way to the last bedroom, the one over the far corner of his study. The door was closed, which was unlike Lindsey, who always kept the doors open. Gripping the glass knob, he opened the door. The hinges squealed like spikes being yanked from a wooden block, a sound that rivaled fingernails scraping across a chalkboard. He wasn't expecting to find anything, but what he discovered gave his heart a sudden jolt.

Wearing a powder-blue bathrobe and matching bedroom slippers, a woman who had to be in her late eighties, stood at the center of the room. Realizing she hadn't spotted him, he watched as she approached his late grandparents' antique dresser and gave it a once-over with an old-fashioned feather duster. Her movements were slow and meticulous, as if she were either in a trance or her mind was stuck in auto drive.

Jake gritted his teeth and clenched his fists. His temper flared. Who was this lady? And what was she doing in their home? Most of all, how did she get inside?

Beads of sweat formed on Jake's brow. Stepping toward her, he stopped cold. The woman was floating completely off the floor. She was no more than ten feet away, so there was no mistaking what he was seeing. Not only was she floating, but he could see *through* her. As he stood frozen, Jake's blood pressure approached the stratosphere. More bad news: this frail-looking, elderly woman cast no reflection in the dresser's mirror.

Jake felt the hair at the back of his neck stand on end. After Vietnam, he'd presumed nothing would ever shock him again. All of a sudden, he realized just how off-base he'd been. Remaining by the door, feeling as if he'd been walloped across his head with a lead pipe, his every thought disintegrated.

It was then that the woman detected him. As she turned, their eyes met and her jaw dropped. Jake watched as she floated across the bedroom—faster than he thought possible. To his astonishment, she disappeared through the interior wall adjacent to the bed.

Jake remained frozen in place. First, it was the lead pipe. Now it felt as if a blast of frigid air had ravaged him, leaving a godawful tingling that chilled him to the bone. He removed his glasses, rubbed his eyes, and then put them back on, all the while feeling his heart performing somersaults. He recalled Mrs. Hampton's remarks about the mansion's ghosts. *Oh, crap! Looks like she wasn't exaggerating after all.*

Peering at the spot on the wall where the woman had disappeared, Jake groaned. His sense of reality had just received a kick in the groin. The woman was something he couldn't explain, not without some ludicrous answer. It wasn't only mind-boggling, it was devastating. Could the real estate agent have been right? Was this house *actually* haunted? And if she *was* right—didn't she say there were *six* ghosts?

Slowly, Jake made his way down the hallway. He felt as if he had been flung head first into a cement mixer. It had been one hell of a day, to say the least. He would shut down the computer, double check the house's locks, and go to bed; although after what he had just seen, his nights of sleeping well were endangered. The elderly woman possessed his every thought. When she had finally spotted him, it was as if he had given *her* a scare. Imagine that? Him giving a *ghost* a fright?

Struggling down the staircase, his bad knee throbbing the entire time, the farthest thing from Jake's mind was the income he would earn owning a bed-and-breakfast facility. What had he done? Had he put Lindsey and Heidi in danger, like Rick had suggested? Or was it logical to presume that ghosts were harmless since they were invisible and couldn't physically *touch* a person? When asked, Mrs. Hampton had answered in a most emphatic manner that they were not dangerous.

With his thoughts coming to a halt, exhaustion set in. It had been a long day and an even longer night. Jake decided to sort the whole thing out in the morning. Hopefully, by then, he would be fresh and better able to think.

***

The wind that swept south through the pass had finally subsided and the mansion had remained quiet for the majority of the night. Then, in the early morning hours, Rick sprang up in bed. Both his heart and lungs were throbbing, and his pillow was moist with sweat. As a screenwriter, he lived and breathed movies but that wasn't necessarily a good thing. Sometimes they infiltrated themselves into his dreams. So now, once again, he'd been dreaming about being chased by flesh-eating zombies. Ever since watching the movie *Night of The Living Dead* at one of those midnight showings at the Portage Theater in his hometown of Chicago, such nightmares had become a regular occurrence.

It took Rick a while to read his watch through the darkness; the digits were bright green but quite small. It was 3:11 a.m. Great, there was plenty of time for some more sleep. With a sprinkler system to install, and who knows what else Jake would come up with, he intended to enjoy his every minute of slumber.

But sleep eluded Rick and he found himself staring at the ceiling. In the darkness it appeared to be a hundred feet away. The bedroom was oddly shaped, half of it inside the gable that faced west. The gabled section appeared similar to most rooms that featured a bay window. At the center stood a battered rocking chair that also seemed to be at least a hundred years old. Cardboard boxes were stacked to the right of the bed. An ornate brass chandelier, which occasionally swung on its own for no apparent reason, hung above him. The room was comfortable enough, he supposed, but he didn't care for the mansion. Recalling the shadowy outline in the mirror, he shuddered. The memory of it troubled him. He hadn't been able to make out the shadow's identity, and now the mere thought of it shriveled his stomach.

Just relax and go to sleep, for crying out loud, snapped a voice in his head. A voice that sounded more like a drill sergeant than his own. *Don't think about zombies, shadowy figures, or swinging chandeliers.*

Rolling over, Rick fluffed his pillow and pulled the blanket up to his shoulder. As he drifted off, an eerie creak roused him.

Half asleep, he turned and peered at the gabled section of the room. In the window a full moon rose into the starless sky, casting a frail illumination into the room. Surreal shadows lurked everywhere. He focused on the rocking chair, undoubtedly the source of the creak. A murky outline scrutinized him from the chair, the moonlight brightly reflected in a pair of narrow eyes.

Rick's breathing ceased. With each beat of his heart, the outline took shape. Someone was in the rocker. Someone who may or may not be human—watched him with unwavering eyes that shone like mirrors through the darkness.

Rising onto his elbows, Rick struggled to swallow. His throat had deteriorated into a barren wasteland. "Who's there?" he croaked. "What do you want?"

No response. Nothing felt right. The room had grown as cold as a tomb. The rocker started moving back and forth, giving rise to a series of creaks that gnawed at his nerves and challenged his sanity.

Rick pushed away the bedding, his eyes locked on the figure. He reached for the nightstand, grabbed the penlight on his keychain, and activated it. The resulting fragile illumination proved all but inadequate.

The creaking halted. The figure of a woman emerged in the rocker, her eyes surveying him with profound interest. Strands of dark, unruly hair draped themselves across the sheerest of negligees, her breasts rising and falling with every breath. Tilting her head, a seductive smirk crossed the woman's pallid face. Her lips parted. Unnerving silence gripped the room. While Rick watched, she raised a leg and ran a hand along her black stocking.

Rick's jaw and everything inside him dropped. His ability to utter a mere syllable had become impossible. His body felt as if it were on fire and sweat drenched his clothing. But most of all, he'd become *aroused*. The woman was stunning, provocative, but in a most lurid manner—like an image from an old pulp magazine. Was he having another nightmare? He knew better. Jake had talked about ghosts. And now one had materialized.

The woman rose to her feet. Her negligee slipped from her

bone-colored shoulders. Her seductive grin transformed into a vision of lust and malice. Floating toward him, she stretched her arms forward. As she closed in, the details of her alluring but hardened face, milky white flesh, and shimmering eyes, crystalized in alarming clarity.

A flood of emotions devastated Rick: a combination of arousal, confusion, and fear. As the woman neared, her flesh disintegrated, revealing rotting organs caged in bone. As she vanished, her eyes lingered for what seemed an eternity, reflecting untold wantonness, anger, and bitterness.

"What the hell!" Rick cried, running a hand through his hair. "What kind of shitstorm was that?"

Taking a panicky breath, he checked his watch. It was 3:17. He'd been awake a full six minutes. A flurry of questions raced through his mind. He forced them back. Only one question was relevant: what did this mean?

Easing onto his pillow, Rick recalled what Jake had mentioned about the mansion. It was supposed to be haunted, a claim they had *both* doubted. When asked, Jake had denied seeing anything out of the ordinary. Sure, the woman *looked* real. But had he just encountered an *actual* ghost? He wanted to scream, *Damn right I did!* But still, he felt conflicted. The truth was that *most* ghostly encounters were explained one way or another. But that word *"most"* bothered him. Could the woman have been a carryover from a dream, an after-dream as it were? If he weren't so horrified, he would laugh out loud.

Rick turned onto his side and decided he was done debating with himself. No matter how much he argued, no matter how much he rationalized, he had either seen an authentic ghost or something more malicious—something evil and *demonic*. He would warn the McKays first thing in the morning. Hopefully, they would believe him. So far they had been spared such terrifying confrontations. Quite frankly, he wouldn't wish something like this on his worst enemy.

Intrusions

By 5:30, Lindsey was in the kitchen making coffee. She had slept horribly, waking up several times during the night. The last time she woke, she had again seen the old woman from the kitchen. Dressed in the same powder-blue bathrobe, the woman had been observing Jake as he slept. When she had noticed that Lindsey was watching her, she had appeared *terrified*. Immediately, she floated across the room, and as Lindsey's gooseflesh gave rise, she vanished not more than eight feet away.

A distinct frigidness filled the bedroom as Lindsey remained sitting upright, stunned beyond words. Who was this woman and what did she want? One supernatural sighting was enough, but two in just half a day? She considered waking Jake but she could just hear him now. "Geez, honey. You were just dreaming. Go back to sleep."

Careful not to wake her husband, Lindsey had climbed out of bed and slipped into her robe. Her heart still pounded and her state of mind had grown jumbled, discouraged, perhaps even mortified. Any more sleep would be out of the question. She may as well get her day started.

After half an hour and two cups of coffee, Lindsey decided to put their current situation behind her for now. She had too much work to do without worrying about ghosts. Besides, so what if the house was haunted? It was obvious that the old woman had been frightened. If she was afraid of a normal, everyday person, then it was reasonable to assume she would be afraid of just about anyone. At the very least, this ghost was harmless. Lindsay's main concern was the blood that had gushed from the faucet. And it hadn't been just rusty water either. She was sure of it. She had smelled and tasted what could only have been blood.

When the time was right, she would mention both the blood *and* the woman to Jake. As she had decided before, the skeptical grinch wouldn't believe her, a fact that could be chiseled in stone. He would attribute these sightings to her mind playing tricks on her—no doubt about that—instigated by Mrs. Hampton's insistence that the house was haunted.

Remembering she had promised her parents photos of their new home, Lindsey retrieved her 35-mm Pentax camera from the kitchen table, a genuine dinosaur in this day and age. Having been into photography since she was ten-years-old, she considered herself "old-school," preferring cameras with rolls of film and manual controls instead of the newfangled digital monstrosities that were starting to come out. Through the years, her Pentax had become her old and trusted friend—a genuine bond that prevented her from discarding it. She still had a dozen shots left, so why not finish the roll while the house was quiet?

With her camera in hand, Lindsey went to work. In each of the downstairs rooms, she lined up each shot with the precision of a professional. Once she was satisfied, she hurried to the basement and photographed her darkroom. She finished what was left on the roll and decided she'd taken enough. Besides, she could hear Heidi talking all the way from her bedroom by way of the newly installed heating ducts. Lindsey chuckled. As her father used to say, "The apple doesn't fall far from the tree." Her daughter was just like her when she was six, talking to herself whenever she was alone.

Lindsey left her camera in the darkroom and hurried up the

stairs to the kitchen. She would fix Heidi breakfast, and before the guys climbed out of bed, she might have enough time to develop the photos.

***

Heidi McKay slept to nearly 6:30, unusual for her. When she woke, she flinched and her eyes bulged. The same little girl she had seen outside was sitting on her bedroom floor. In the little girl's hands was Heidi's favorite Barbie doll, the one wearing the prom dress.

Jumping out of bed, Heidi joined the girl, who didn't run away this time. "Hi, I'm so glad you're here. I thought I'd never see you again." Kneeling on the floor, she peered at the bedroom door. "What are you doing here so early? Did Mommy let you in?"

Seemingly oblivious, the girl remained quiet, her eyes locked on the doll in her hands, as if she'd never seen one before.

"That's Barbie," Heidi murmured. "I have three of them."

At long last the little girl looked up from the doll. Her large brown eyes were both striking and captivating. Perfect ringlets of golden hair cascaded across her frail shoulders. Her lips seemed frozen in an innocent but pouty expression. She wore the same summer dress as before, with a slightly tattered hem.

"What's your name?" Heidi asked.

For a long, lingering moment, a cautious expression crept into the girl's eyes. Her answer should have struck the six-year-old as odd. Perhaps even sinister. But in her enthusiasm to make friends, Heidi was willing to overlook just about anything. As the girl responded, she could hear her well enough but her voice sounded distorted. Stranger still, her lips never moved. "I'm Victoria Mayfield," she answered. "Vicki for short."

"Hi, Vicki, I'm Heidi." Smiling, the six-year-old held out her hand.

Victoria cringed and her dark eyes grew enormous. "Oh, no. We must *never* touch!"

Taken by surprise, Heidi's mouth dropped. "Why not?"

Her lips pouting all the more, the little girl appeared to mull the question over. Finally, she answered. "It wouldn't be proper."

Heidi shrugged. She didn't understand but decided to drop the subject for now. In fear of making her new friend run away again, she also decided not to ask why her lips didn't move when she spoke. "Will you play with me? We can be friends. You'd be my *first* friend since we moved here."

Glancing at the doll, Victoria appeared hesitant.

"Please, Vicki, we'll have fun, and I have lots of dolls to play with."

"There's something I must tell you first," Victoria whispered in an earnest manner. "Something important."

Heidi eased into a sitting position, crossed her legs, and probed, "Sure. What is it?"

Victoria began unraveling a most incredible secret. So incredible that no one but a six-year-old would believe it.

***

Lindsey had put Heidi's bowl of cereal on the kitchen table, along with milk and a glass of apple juice. She hurried up the stairs, poked her head into her daughter's bedroom, and told her to get dressed and come for breakfast. Heidi was on the floor playing with her dolls, which wasn't unusual. The fact that she appeared annoyed at the request, however, seemed strange. It felt to Lindsay as if she wasn't welcome just then and that her presence was an intrusion.

***

Lindsey sat at the kitchen table, sipping coffee and watching Heidi eat her bowl of cereal.

"Can I go out and play, Mommy?" her daughter asked, finishing.

"You want to go outside *this early?*"

"Of course," Heidi answered emphatically. "Maybe I'll see Victoria."

Setting her coffee aside, a bewildered Lindsey peered at her daughter, who looked as if she had just let a ferocious old alley cat out of the bag. "Victoria? Who's Victoria?"

"She's my new friend," replied Heidi with more than a hint of hesitation. "She's very sweet. I mostly call her Vicki."

Lindsey felt a lump forming at the back of her throat. She didn't know why, but a bad feeling had just crept in. "You made a friend? Out *here*? At this place? When did you meet her?"

Apparently sensing her mother's concern, Heidi shrugged. "Some time yesterday. It's a secret, and I'm not supposed to tell anyone." Frowning, she stared at the table. "She's not—" She took a deep breath. "Not like my old friends. She's different."

Lindsey sat motionless, trying to sort through her daughter's response. There wasn't another house around for at least a mile. How could she have met anyone new when she was home all day? Was Vicki an imaginary friend? Lindsey felt a tinge of guilt. Perhaps she should be awarded a trophy with the inscription "Worst Mother of the Year." Dragging an only child away from her friends would certainly qualify her for such a dishonor.

"Can I go out now, Mommy?" Heidi persisted. "Please?"

Lindsey was about to answer when the telephone rang, the first time since they had moved in. She had to postpone their conversation and answer it or the ringing would wake Jake and Rick. "Okay," she responded, rising to her feet. "But stay close to the house. We don't want any more episodes with rattlesnakes."

Heidi rushed off as Lindsey hurried to the wall phone. When she picked up the receiver, the caller disconnected, but only after a long, awkward silence. Disappointed, Lindsey hung up. She had been hoping it was either her mom or sister. Taking a final sip of coffee, she peered at her watch. It was just after seven. Because he had tossed and turned most of the night, Jake would be asleep for at least another hour, and Rick was notorious for sleeping late. If she skipped washing dishes for now, there was still time to develop her film.

***

By 8:20, Lindsey was in the final stages of developing the photos of their new home. First, in a small, plastic, lightproof jar, she had soaked the film in developer solution. Next, using the same jar, she rinsed the film in a stop bath that included acetic acid and then applied a fixer solution. While the film was in her electric dryer, she set up three metal pans of the same chemicals: developer, stop bath, and fixer solution. Next, she cut the negatives using scissors and, using her old, trusty enlarger, processed the film onto Kodak Grade 2 paper. Slipping on a pair of rubber gloves, she soaked each of the 8 by 10 prints in her metal pans. When the soaking process was completed, she would hang the results to dry on the nylon cord she had hung along the top shelf.

Lindsey had developed her own photos since she was seventeen. Of course, she used only black and white format, as developing color prints had proven too complicated. The 6-foot by 10-foot basement storage closet had proved to be a nearly perfect location for her darkroom. There were no windows, and it had built-in shelves from front to back and two electrical sockets. When Mrs. Hampton had shown them the basement closet, Lindsey couldn't believe her luck. The room was a dream come true. With the three-foot-deep shelves, there was plenty of space to fasten down both the photograph dryer and the enlarger. But there were drawbacks as well: the room had no insulation and would grow cold and stuffy very quickly, plus it was on the small side, making her work environment cramped.

Completing the last of the photos, Lindsey noticed something peculiar in the wide-angle shot of the living room. To the right of the fireplace was a fairly large, murky blur. It was translucent with no definite form. From what she recalled from one of her many high school science projects, it looked like an amoeba under a microscope lens.

Lindsey knew the roll of film hadn't been exposed, as all the other pictures came out fine. Besides, exposed film didn't look like that. She recalled the old woman wearing the powder-blue bathrobe. Could this be what a ghost looked like when caught on slow-speed, black-and-white film? If this image did turn out to be a ghost, what an incredible discovery. The photo would not only prove their existence—but might even become famous.

***

Heidi had been playing knucklebones—commonly known as jacks—on a bare, hard piece of ground for over ten minutes. It was still early but already the morning was warming up. As she grew more and more bored with the game, she sensed someone watching her. Spinning around, she discovered Victoria sitting on the porch step. "Hi, Vicki! Want to play jacks?"

The little girl nodded and joined her on the ground. Vicki said she didn't know how to play, so Heidi explained. It felt good to be playing with someone, and Heidi looked forward to spending the whole day with her new friend.

***

Jake was awakened by an annoying sound. First, there was a bump followed by a squeak, and then another bump and another squeak. Tired from not sleeping well, at first he tried ignoring it and even covered his head with a pillow. Nevertheless, the noise persisted, traveling up and down the hallway just outside his bedroom door. Who could be making such a racket? Grumbling, he decided he'd had enough. It was almost 8:30 anyway and he couldn't sleep his life away.

Snatching his glasses from the nightstand, Jake climbed out of bed. Not yet fully awake, he stumbled his way across the room and opened the bedroom door, which oddly enough had been closed once again. He stuck his head out into the hallway. The corridor was empty and the sound had stopped.

Another ghost? No way. Older homes were full of creaks and groans. And how could a ghost make noises? Having no bodies, they shouldn't be able to make any type of sound. There were probably half a dozen explanations for what he was hearing, but at the moment he couldn't think of any.

Jake went to the bathroom and then washed up. He would

take a shower later, as soon as he had a chance to check on Lindsey and Heidi. Returning to the bedroom, he threw on a pair of old jeans, his favorite T-shirt—the one with the L.A. Rams logo—and hurried down the staircase. Since Rick's bedroom door was closed, more than likely his friend was still sleeping. Well good, at least someone in this house was having some quality time.

Making his way down the staircase, Jake had to remind himself to use the banister. His knee pain was on the mild side this morning, but the joint flexibility was never good.

As Jake entered the kitchen, the aroma of fresh coffee greeted him. A broad smile spread across his face. Caffeine and tobacco were his only vices. Back in his Vietnam days, he had smoked grass and drank more than his share of liquor. Nowadays, he still had an occasional beer, especially when Rick was around, but marijuana was a thing of the past. One of these days he would quit smoking altogether. He blamed his father's premature death on cigarettes. But caffeine? That was another matter. Coffee was his connection to the land of "Happy-go-lucky Jake," as Lindsey had often teased him. Without it, he would be condemned to the world of "Grouchy Jake," also coined by Lindsey, and his everyday functioning would be at gutter level.

Jake headed straight toward the coffeemaker, looking forward to his first cup. He discovered a note from Lindsey on the counter. Grabbing an extra-large mug from the nearby cabinet, he poured himself a cup and read the note. His wife was working in her darkroom and wanted him to check on Heidi, who was outside. Breakfast would be ready around nine.

Setting down the note, Jake took another gulp and stepped over to the window by the sink. He could see his daughter not more than sixty feet away, sitting on the ground, playing jacks.

He yawned and ran a hand through his beard. If only he'd slept better. He decided he would take a look at the morning newspaper, keep checking on Heidi, and wait for Rick to get his butt out of bed. They would have breakfast together and then it would be back to the sprinkler system. But before long, he had to talk to Lindsey about the little old lady he'd encountered. The ghost in the powder-blue bathrobe. He didn't mind sharing the account with Rick, too, but thought better of telling Heidi. Their daughter was much too impressionable, even at her age.

***

Heidi had been playing with her new friend, Vicki, making all kinds of conversation. It was all just small talk to the six-year-old, but the discussion was anything but casual. Scooping up a jack, she asked the little girl if the story she had told her earlier was true.

Vicki nodded, a solemn expression settling on her face. "Every word," she whispered.

Heidi stared at her playmate for a while then asked, "If your story is true, then you're dead, right?"

Again, the little girl nodded.

Bouncing the ball, Heidi scored another jack. "If you're dead, then . . . what are you?"

Vicki stared at Heidi for some time. When she finally answered, once again her lips didn't move. "I'm a ghost," she declared. "Mother says we both are."

Glancing to Vicki, Heidi missed the ball and it bounced across the yard. "Should I be scared?"

The little girl shook her head. "Don't be scared. None of us will hurt you . . . none of us except—" Vicki stopped speaking as she looked over Heidi's shoulder. Her expression changed from somber to fearful.

Suddenly, Heidi realized there was something just behind them, something that was frightening her new friend. She turned around. Except for the house, which looked *especially* huge from the ground, there wasn't anything to be seen. Glancing back, she spotted her friend running toward the back of the garage once again. Her heart sank and her mood plunged. Everything had been going so well until now. "Vicki, wait! What's wrong? I didn't see anything." The six-year-old sprang to her feet, her heart skipping a beat. Despite what her parents had told her, she hurried to the other side of the garage. Scanning the apple orchard, she didn't see her friend. Now why would she run off like that? And what could have frightened her?

Turning, Heidi approached the old refrigerator. How strange. The door was open but she remembered shutting it yesterday. It wasn't likely that her mommy or daddy had opened it. As far as the six-year-old knew, they didn't even know the thing existed. Perhaps Vicki was hiding inside and hadn't had the chance to close the door.

Rushing to the front of the refrigerator, Heidi was struck with discouragement. The darn thing was empty. Just brown stains inside. She shrugged and again thought of Vicki. She had looked terrified, as if she had just seen something horrible. Was it a ghost? It must have been. But why would a ghost be afraid of another ghost? Because it was mean and did bad things?

A pair of sounds came rushing up from behind: solid thuds against the ground and coarse breathing. As Heidi started to turn around, something shoved her hard and she fell into the refrigerator, striking her head on the back wall. She cried out in shock and pain. The air inside tasted bitter and rotten. The coarse breathing became harder, heavier and constant; she couldn't tell if it was a person or an animal. Her arms and legs were grabbed by what felt like strong hands, which stuffed all of her limbs into the interior. She cried and screamed and thrashed about, all the while unable to see what was forcing her into the tiny space.

Before Heidi could climb out, the door slammed shut and everything turned black.

The Darkroom

Lindsey was nearly finished in the darkroom. The only thing left to do was to dispose the contents of the pans. She would pour the chemicals into plastic bottles, and as soon as she had the chance, drop them off at the hazardous waste site.

Working beneath an infrared light had always felt ominous. It tended to distort the surroundings. Murky shadows gathered in the corners, across the floor, and on the shelves. She'd always thought the illumination had an otherworldliness to it. Realizing their new home was haunted only magnified her discomfort. Although she had enjoyed developing the photos, once she'd spotted the blur, a dreadful eeriness overcame her. A sort of instinct, for the lack of a better word, that she suspected she had inherited from her maternal grandmother, a Navajo medicine woman who could read fortunes when the stars were "in proper alignment." The darkroom had grown more and more sinister, and she felt as if she were the proverbial mouse wandering around in the snake's lair. And there was more. For the last twenty minutes or so, she could not shake the sensation that she was being watched, and the longer she worked, the more persistent the feeling became.

Lindsey pushed herself to finish. She had to hurry. She wanted to be out in the light of day. As she was about to drain the pans, the chemicals inside them began churning. She flinched and stepped back. What could *possibly* cause such a thing? An earthquake? No, definitely not. Everything else in the room remained stationary—and the floor wasn't quivering. Something else had to be causing it.

Stunned by a mixture of confusion and trepidation, Lindsey inched toward the door. The churning escalated and the chemicals began splashing onto the shelves. Afraid to take her eyes away from the pans, she reached for the doorknob and started to pull. But as the door began to open, it was yanked back from the other side. "What in the world?"

Again, Lindsey tried opening the door, but it wouldn't budge. Someone had to be on the other side holding it shut. There was no other explanation.

All three pans were rocking violently, so much so that she could hear them banging against the shelf. Wrestling with a fear she had never known before, Lindsey turned toward them, trying to decide what to do. She turned just in time to see the pans jump off the shelf and fly at her. Before they struck, she raised her arms and shut her eyes. The pans bounced off her arms and landed on the floor, sending a metallic clatter through the room.

Cold, cruel reality struck, filling Lindsey with dread. She was soaked to the skin in acid. Her face, hair, and arms were drenched. Flinging her hair back, she returned to the door and tried to pull it open. Again, someone had to be holding it shut, someone much stronger than her.

Adding to her horror, the acids were beginning to burn. She called for Jake and Rick but there was no answer. They were probably upstairs, but because sound traveled so well through the heating ducts, there was a chance they could hear if she kept trying. Banging on the door, she screamed, "Damn you! Move away and let me out of here!" A growing sense of desperation erupted inside her. Although the door opened from the inside, she stepped back and tried ramming it. All she accomplished was driving a bolt of pain through her shoulder.

Fear swelled into panic. She punched the door with her fists as hard as she could, scraping and bloodying her knuckles. "Let me out, damn you! Let me out!" There was no response. The door remained shut. She was trapped and her body—from her face to her knees—were starting to burn.

***

Exhausted, Heidi kept trying to open the refrigerator door. She'd been screaming for help and banging on the walls to no avail. With each passing minute, she grew weaker. The heat had become unbearable, and she could no longer take a full breath. The more she struggled, the harder it was for her to breathe.

The instant the door had closed, total blackness had engulfed her. She'd never been in such dreadful darkness, where she was completely stripped of sight. She'd always been frightened of the dark, and in her young mind, darkness had become the condition that preceded death. She'd heard that children her age didn't understand death, but not her, not since her cat, Mandy, had been hit by a car last year. She understood death perfectly and the notion terrified her.

No matter how much Heidi tried to stay calm, she couldn't, and before long, tears drenched her face. How was she going to get out? Where were her parents? And where could Vicki be? Vicki was her friend and should be helping her.

Just as hope faded, Heidi heard a voice, barely audible, but a voice just the same. She didn't understand why, but she heard it within the deepest regions of her mind: a soft, soothing voice assuring her that everything would be all right. Someone was nearby, but would they be able to open the refrigerator door? At any moment now she would no longer be able to breathe.

Too weak to utter anything but a gasp, Heidi was about to lose consciousness. She was running out of time. Whoever was close by had better hurry. Opening the door would save her, and she *desperately* wanted to live. She wanted to be with her mom and dad. To hug them and kiss them. She couldn't bear the thought of dying. *Please, hurry,* she begged. *Please open the . . .*

***

It wasn't easy to contain her panic, but Lindsey summoned every ounce of courage and held onto it with stubborn determination. Keeping her breathing under control, she focused herself. Using her body as a battering ram and slamming into the door would not help, and she knew that whoever was holding the door shut was much stronger than her. Because of the chemicals, she didn't have much time. Although inhibited by their prolonged use during the developing process, the acids were still strong enough to burn. Not an intense burning as of yet, but it would be increasing soon enough. If she didn't do something quickly, she could be scarred for life.

Suddenly, Lindsey knew what to do. She kept a gallon of distilled water on the bottom shelf for diluting the chemicals. Why hadn't she thought of it before? Dropping to her knees, she snatched the jug. Thank God, in just a few more seconds she would be able to neutralize the acid, then she could concentrate on getting out of the darkroom.

Her revelry took a sudden reversal when the cap refused to budge. Cursing, Lindsey closed her eyes and steadied her hands. Breathing through gritted teeth, she twisted the cap as hard as she could. As she struggled, she could feel the acid burning her face, arms, and chest. "It has to open," she uttered, her voice frantic. "It has to come off!"

When the cap gave way, there was no time to waste. Lifting the bottle over her head, she poured the entire contents over herself. Lukewarm water cascaded down her body, dissipating the burning. Relief consumed her. Sweet, *glorious* relief.

Soaked from head to foot, Lindsey set the jug down. As she was about to reach for the door, someone knocked on the other side. A knocking that was soft and hesitant. Not knowing who or what she would discover, she swallowed and took an anxious breath. Trembling, she gave the doorknob a timid pull. The door creaked open without effort.

Jake stood in front of her, a bewildered expression plastered across his face, his eyes nearly bulging out of their sockets. Staring at her, he appeared oblivious to the fact that she was kneeling on the floor, soaked to the skin. "Honey, you're not going to believe this," he whispered after an awkward silence, his eyes unblinking. "But Mrs. Hampton was right. This house is *definitely* haunted."

Lindsey grabbed the lower shelf for support and rose to her feet. Her legs wobbled, her knees nearly buckled, and she struggled to catch her breath. Despite keeping her emotions in check, she had to fight the urge not to smack her husband on the head with one of the pans. Not that she was a violent person, but her frustration was teetering at the brink. "No kidding?" she snarled, her tone indignant. "What makes you say that?"

"I-I saw something—"

A disturbing sense of reality swept through Lindsey. She gasped out loud and grabbed her husband by the arms, causing him to jump back. "Have you checked on Heidi? Is she all right?"

A virtual road map of wrinkles formed on Jake's brow. "Well, yeah, a few minutes ago. She's okay. Playing jacks behind the house."

Pushing past him, Lindsey raced toward the stairs. Jake followed her as they sprinted through the house. She headed for the kitchen window over the sink, her instincts in an uproar, expecting to find every mother's most dreaded fear—that her child was in mortal danger.

Lindsey reached the kitchen window and flung back the drape. Once again, relief surged through her. Heidi was sitting on one of the swings, appearing calm, innocent, and most of all safe, while holding a wilted dandelion in her hand.

Jake came up from behind and looked over his wife's shoulder. "You see, honey. She's fine. Never better. Just like I told you."

A flood of emotions overwhelmed Lindsey. She'd been controlling them, but when it came to her only child, they were all but uncontrollable. Her head felt like a ball bouncing around inside a pinball machine. Her heart still raced as if she'd been running a marathon. Something felt wrong. Something told her that when it came to Heidi, both she and Jake had fallen into a false sense of security. She leaned against the counter, inhaled deeply, then exhaled. Anything that resembled a *true* sense of relief vanished. Through the years she had learned to listen to her instincts, which had always been spot on. Heidi was safe for the time being—*but for how long*?

Lindsay gazed at Jake. He was standing beside her, his eyes anxious, looking up and down her soaked body. "Honey," he murmured. "What happened in the darkroom?"

With her throat parched, her thoughts focused elsewhere, she tried to respond by saying, "Something tried to kill me," but the words never left her.

Her concern for her own wellbeing had to be put on hold. Her daughter was, and would always be, her focus. Yes, Heidi was okay for now. Yet a variety of deep-seated feelings nagged Lindsey, sending shudders up her spine. With each passing moment they grew stronger, rising to her consciousness, proclaiming Heidi was in danger. In fact, they were *all* in danger and anything, literally *anything,* could happen.

The Unseen

While Lindsey showered, Jake told her about the elderly ghost he'd encountered. He described what she was wearing and that she had been dusting their furniture, an obsession if he ever saw one. He finished by describing how the woman had floated away and disappeared through a wall. As Lindsey watched him through the shower's glass door, he stepped into their bedroom and sat on the edge of the bed. Staring out the window, he appeared to be calming himself.

Lindsey scrubbed off any traces of acid, no matter how small, and was greatly relieved to see she wasn't scarred. The skin on her upper chest had turned a faint shade of red, but otherwise, she was fine—physically, anyway. Thank God for the distilled water and that the acids had been diluted in the first place. Lindsey groaned and shook her head. She hated "what ifs." They weren't based in reality and a person could go out of their minds dwelling on them. But nevertheless, *what if* . . . the acids had splattered into her *eyes*? Or into her mouth? She shivered. If she ever wanted to sleep at night, she'd better forget about the "what ifs."

After drying off and slipping into her bathrobe, Lindsey

hurried into the bedroom, eyeing the hairbrush on the dresser. Hunched over, Jake was sitting on the far corner of the bed, still staring out the window, his brow furrowed in wrinkles. Her heart sank. She could swear that the gray hairs in his beard had doubled overnight. She knew her husband. He was upset and feeling guilty about moving them into the mansion.

"Cheer up, I'll make some breakfast and we'll talk," she said, brushing her hair and looking into the dresser's mirror. She couldn't believe it. Not that she needed to, but she'd lost weight. Apparently, living with ghosts had negative effects on both Jake and her. She rolled her eyes and gazed at her reflection in the mirror. "You're not alone in this," she confessed. "I have a few stories of my own."

Jake straightened. More wrinkles appeared. "Like what happened in your darkroom?"

Lindsey nodded. "That . . . and *a lot* more." She chuckled. Fifteen minutes ago, she had wanted to smack the guy in the head. Now she wanted to hug him. "Come on, let's talk while we eat."

Leaving the bedroom, they ran into Rick coming out of the "Thomas Jefferson" guest room. According to Mrs. Hampton, each of the rooms had been given names by the original owner, mostly of former presidents. The master bedroom was coined "the George Washington Chamber." Heidi's bedroom was called "the James Madison Quarters." Jake's office, however, was an exception. It was called "the Hamilton Study," as in Alexander Hamilton. Lindsey thought the whole idea sounded ludicrous. After they had moved in, she suggested renaming the rooms after Heidi's favorite Muppet characters. Their daughter would certainly get a kick out of it. The "Kermit Zone" could be Jake's office, and Heidi's bedroom could be called "Miss Piggy's Boudoir." Of course, she was kidding, but Jake didn't know that.

Rick appeared to be doing his best to come across as happy, refreshed, and vibrant. But his eyes spoke differently. Lindsey suspected something had happened to him as well.

"Good morning!" he greeted. "Sorry for sleeping so late." He glanced at Jake and then at Lindsey. His eyes had never been more wary. "So what's been happening? I don't suppose I've missed anything, have I?"

Lindsey gave her husband a bewildered look. Jake forced a grin and took his friend by the arm. "Come on, Uncle Rick. We'll get you caught up."

***

Lindsey called her daughter to come inside, but still full from her bowl of cereal, the six-year-old begged to stay in the back yard. Heidi didn't mention that her new friend, Vicki, had once again joined her or that she was still recovering from being locked in the refrigerator. Lindsey wanted to talk to Heidi to see if anything unusual had happened to her, but her daughter seemed to be enjoying herself, so why spoil it? A few more minutes wouldn't matter. She told Heidi okay but reminded her to stay close to the rear of the house where they could watch her.

Due to the latest restriction because of the rattlesnake, the six-year-old didn't want to tell her parents about being locked in the refrigerator. The ordeal was the scariest thing that had ever happened to her, but it was over, a lesson learned, and it would never happen again. In the future she would avoid any broken-down refrigerators, avoid them as if they were flesh-eating dinosaurs. As far as she was concerned, a mob of grown men couldn't drag her near one.

***

While keeping an eye on Heidi through the kitchen window, Lindsey fried nearly an entire package of bacon. When the bacon was good and crisp, she started the eggs and tossed four slices of bread into the toaster. Before long, the kitchen teemed with the aromas of a hearty breakfast.

Setting full plates before the two men, Lindsey tightened the sash of her robe and joined them. She was still trying to cope with what had happened. Everything had been fine until yesterday, but now things had turned deadly. Seeing a ghost of a little old lady was one thing, but being doused with acid was another. There was a force prowling around in their home, a powerful one at that, and it wanted them dead—or if nothing else, for them to move out. Weren't ghosts supposed to be harmless? She groaned. At least one of them wasn't.

"Well, sweetheart," Jake began, buttering his toast. "Are you going to tell us what's going on or are you going to keep us in suspense?"

Rick glanced over with keen interest.

Lindsey took a nervous breath and exhaled. "I saw the elderly woman too, Jake. I saw her *twice*, and she was wearing the same bathrobe you described."

Jake froze, his eyes wide behind his lenses. "Was she about eighty years old?"

"Probably around ninety, and she looked surprised, if not *shocked*, to see me."

"So that's just one harmless ghost. Right?"

"Ghost?" croaked Rick. "You both saw a ghost?"

"There's supposed to be at least six of them, according to Mrs. Hampton. The old lady's just one." Ignoring her breakfast, Lindsey sipped coffee. "There's something else you should know. Yesterday, when I turned on the kitchen faucet, blood spurted out."

Jake shook his head. "Now, honey, that's just rusty water. It's an old house and the contractor probably never replaced the plumbing."

Setting her cup down, Lindsey released a rather terse sigh. "No, Jake. The contractor *did* replace the plumbing. It said so in the escrow documents. And what came out of the faucet was *blood*. I should know, because I rinsed my face in it." She paused and took another sip of coffee. "Then there's this strange noise—"

Jake swallowed and Lindsey thought his Adam's apple would never come down. He cleared his throat then asked, "A kind of bump, followed by a squeak?"

"That's it exactly! All these occurrences can't be just *one* ghost, and I don't think the old woman would do anything to harm us. So it's my guess there has to be at least two more of them."

Jake cringed and squirmed in his chair. "Okay, but let's get down to what happened in your darkroom."

Lindsey locked eyes with her husband. "All three of my chemical pans started shaking on their own. Then they flew at me . . . as if someone had thrown them, but no one was there. And then the door wouldn't open." Lindsey shuddered, set her coffee down, and lowered her voice. "It started to . . . but it was *pulled* back. Here I was soaked with chemicals that contained a mixture of acid, and I couldn't get out of the room. I'm *positive* someone was behind that door. Someone who none of us can see. A *powerful* force who is trying to make us move out—or murder us if we don't."

Rick set his fork down. "So to be clear, you're saying one of these ghosts threw acid on you in an attempt to kill you?"

Folding her arms, Lindsey nodded. "Yeah, it was doing its darndest . . . until Jake showed up."

Her husband groaned. "I didn't see anything holding the door, honey. I saw the old woman last night, but when I approached the darkroom, there was nothing there."

"I didn't see it either when it threw the pans at me. That ghost is different than the woman. I think it's *intentionally* hiding itself." Lindsey rubbed her forehead. "The woman, and maybe the rest of them, are more visible, especially when you catch them *off guard*, when they don't know you're seeing them . . . that's when they're vulnerable."

Her eyes lit up and she shot to her feet. "I almost forgot!" Setting her coffee cup on the counter, she rushed toward the basement door. "Stay put. Both of you. There's something I want you to see."

***

While Vicki stood off to the left, Heidi continued swinging at a slow, steady rate. The old swing set creaked and groaned as if it was complaining. Heidi had tried to get her friend to join in, but Vicki would have no part of it.

"So you're not really six-years-old, right?" Heidi asked.

The little girl shook her head. "No. I don't know my age."

Slowing the swing even further, Heidi asked, "What year were you born?"

Vicki frowned and appeared to think about the question, then answered, "1941."

Heidi's mouth dropped. "Boy, Vicki, you're old!"

The girl shrugged. "No, I'm not. I'm young."

"Not if you were born that long ago!"

With her mouth suddenly ajar, Vicki began backing away. Alarmed once again, she was staring toward the house.

"What's wrong?" Heidi jumped off the swing, nearly stumbling onto the hard, unforgiving ground.

"He's coming," her friend warned. "You'd better hide. You'd better hide right away." With that she turned toward the garage and vanished.

"Don't go," a discouraged Heidi pleaded. "He can't really hurt us, can he?"

But her friend was gone, disappearing to wherever ghosts go when they don't want to be seen. And it was all for nothing, as Heidi couldn't see a ghost, or anything else for that matter. Except for a mild breeze caressing her face, it seemed as if the entire desert had come to a standstill.

Returning to the playset, the six-year-old plopped down on the middle swing. Gazing at the ground, a sense of loneliness made itself know. She hated feeling that way. Being the only child in the middle of nowhere was like a terrible punishment that was way too mean.

A long, sad sigh escaped Heidi as she kicked the ground. To her surprise, she heard footsteps. She turned but couldn't see anyone. Was she hearing things? She didn't think so. Not with a bunch of ghosts running around. She recalled the footsteps that she had heard just before being pushed into the refrigerator and her whole body quivered. But those were *loud* footsteps, she recalled, plus there was that coarse breathing that came with it.

It was then that Heidi was given a delicate push. Her mood lightened. Holding onto the swing's chains, she allowed herself to be gently propelled, all the while giggling appreciatively.

Vicki had returned. Perhaps she was still frightened and was staying invisible, but she was there just the same. Happy to have her friend back, Heidi giggled some more. She allowed her friend to push her harder, and as usual the playset squeaked and moaned.

***

Jake and Rick examined the photo Lindsey had placed on the kitchen table, an 8-by-10, black-and-white of the living room. It would have been just an ordinary photograph except for the blur on the right-hand side. It was difficult to determine due to the lack of scale, but Jake guessed the image was a foot in diameter, had no real shape, was transparent, and barely perceptible. To him it resembled a cloud, or a patch of fog.

"Some defect in the film?" ventured Rick.

"No," Lindsey answered, nibbling on a slice of toast. "The rest of the film was fine, and it's not like any flaw I've ever seen."

Rick leaned back and crossed his arms. "Maybe there was a spot on your camera lens."

"No way," Lindsey answered, shaking her head. "I just cleaned the lens."

Jake frowned and toyed with his placemat. "It's probably nothing, honey. An overexposure of some sort or one of a dozen other explanations."

Lindsey stood and poured herself some more coffee. Engrossed in the conversation, she forgot to check on Heidi. "Under normal circumstances, I would agree with you, Jake, but since both of us have witnessed some pretty strange stuff around here, I think we have a photograph of a ghost . . . or at least what they look like when we can't see them."

Taking an uneasy breath, Rick cleared his throat. "There's something I'd better tell you guys."

Lindsey flashed a sly and knowing grin. "Uncle Rick, is there something you'd like to get off your chest? Like seeing a ghost, perhaps?"

Shrugging, he nodded. "I guess so. At first I thought it was a dream, but now I know otherwise." He winced and ran a hand through his thick hair. "It's funny how people tend to rationalize. I even thought I was imagining things." He glanced at Jake, arched an eyebrow, and cracked a smile. "But last night I met a most *provocative* ghost."

Trying to maintain a straight face, Jake leaned forward. "Really? Provocative? What took you so long to tell us?"

Again, his friend shrugged. "I wanted to hear what you guys had to say first. It's not like I was holding out or anything."

Jake rubbed his palms together. "Okay, tell us more, you old rascal. And leave nothing out."

***

With each and every push, Heidi climbed higher. Normally she would have told Vicki to stop, but the six-year-old was more concerned about looking like a crybaby in front of her new friend than how high she traveled.

Every few seconds, Heidi would turn to look but couldn't see anyone. Why didn't Vicki show herself? Obviously, she was there, as she could feel a pair of hands upon her back, so *someone* was pushing her.

Suddenly, Heidi was afraid. She was swinging much too high. She could hear the swing set creaking louder with each passing second. Her arms were aching from holding on so tightly and her heart felt as if it would beat itself to death. "Vicki, that's enough!" the six-year-old hollered.

The pushing not only continued but suddenly she was being pushed even harder. To Heidi's growing terror, her swing had climbed so high, it was now parallel to the top of the playset. The chains she so desperately held onto were bucking and she could barely hold on. She clamped her eyes shut and took the longest breath of her life.

"Victoria, stop," she screamed. "STOP!"

***

"Well, I don't know, Uncle Rick," mused Jake after listening to his friend's encounter with the seductive ghost. "I think you were probably dreaming." Then he added with a wink and a grin, "Or engaging in some *perverted* fantasy."

Rick frowned and grumbled, "Very, funny, Uncle Jake. I knew you were going to give me a hard time."

Finishing her coffee, Lindsey shook her head. "It was real. After all, there's supposed to be *six* ghosts in our mansion. Now with the old woman, that makes two, plus there's the blood from the faucet and that strange noise, the bump followed by a squeak."

Rick sat back. "You know, my nephew just might be able to help. Eats up this kind of stuff like there's no tomorrow." He paused and again arched an eyebrow. "But I have to warn you, he's about twenty thousand miles *beyond* left field . . . and that's putting it mildly." He hesitated and appeared to weigh his every word. "But on the other hand, he's a certified genius if there ever was one. The kid's obsessed with anything that has to do with ghosts, spirits, bogeymen, or whatever." He peered at a less-than-enthusiastic Jake. "Even if he can't help, he knows *a lot* of people who can."

Jake folded his arms across his chest. "Sounds like he could be more trouble than he's worth."

Lindsey cleared her throat. "Okay, let's stay on track, shall we? All three of us have experienced *supernatural* encounters," she summarized, setting her coffee cup on the counter. Turning toward her husband and Rick, all semblance of color suddenly abandoned her face. "And if that's the case . . . then what about Heidi?"

Jake jumped to his feet, his eyes on fire. "She *must* have experienced something."

The three of them rushed toward the window over the sink. It was then that the screaming started—the most blood-curdling sound imaginable. Lindsey, Jake, and Rick were ill-prepared for the sight that played out before their eyes, a sight so horrific that they bolted in unison toward the back yard door.

***

Lindsey led the way, running at breakneck speed. Halfway to the swing set, she stumbled, and despite his bad knee, Jake passed her and reached Heidi first. The six-year-old was being thrust nearly eight feet into the air. Worse yet was the momentum—their daughter had become nothing more than a blur. Jake's every thought focused on saving her—so much so that he couldn't comprehend what she was screaming.

"Sarah, help me!" she pleaded. "Please, Sarah! Save me!"

Jake maneuvered to the rear of the swing set, determined to grab Heidi from behind. He could only hope he'd be able to catch her without either of them being injured. As he neared, an unseen force plowed into him. His legs were thrust upward, sending him soaring through the air. He slammed into the ground and landed on his back, which purged his lungs of air. Excruciating pain incapacitated him. Time slowed to a crawl. All he could do was look at the blur that was his daughter. He'd been flung into a world of helplessness—a stupor where reality no longer existed. No longer mattered. As Rick lunged toward Heidi, Jake watched as if he were in another dimension.

From nowhere, the unseen force struck again. The sight of his friend being rammed as he leaped toward the six-year-old escalated Jake's torment. Rick had *literally bounced*—as if he'd hit a brick wall. He suffered what must have been a brutal mauling as he skidded on his belly across a patch of gravel, came to an abrupt halt, and remained motionless.

Jake returned his attention to the swing set and spotted the cement footings: the metal frame was wrenching loose. He had to get to his feet. He had to rescue his daughter. *Get the hell up,* he demanded, battling his paralysis. He forced himself to his knees and everything around him became a blinding glare. The only thing he could make out was his wife rushing toward the playset.

As Heidi began her backward descent, Lindsey leapt forward and locked her arms around the screaming child. Dragging her feet across the ground, she reduced the runaway swing to a wobble.

Jake gasped and his eyes welled with tears. Thank God, the crisis had been routed. With her arms locked around their six-year-old, Lindsey secured her footing. Kissing and hugging the young girl, she removed her from the swing. "Baby, are you okay?" she asked repeatedly.

Jake's stupor dissipated. He wanted to make sure he wasn't crazy. Gathering his strength, he scanned the area around the playset. Just as he'd thought, there was no visible evidence of what had endangered Heidi and ambushed him and Rick. No man, beast, or ghost—nothing to pinpoint what had caused all this pain, danger, and helplessness.

Exhausted, Jake struggled to his feet, staggered to his wife and daughter, and gave them a hug. They hugged him in return, eagerly, without hesitation, tears flowing from Heidi's eyes, Lindsey trembling in his arms. "Are you guys all right?" he whispered, out of breath.

Still shaken, Lindsey and Heidi nodded.

"Thank God," he murmured. "I was *paralyzed.* I hit the ground so hard . . . I couldn't get up." He released them, wiped the sweat from his forehead, and shuffled toward his friend, who was still sprawled face down on the ground. "Are you okay?" he asked, stooping.

Rick removed a piece of gravel from his bottom lip. "Never better, but I'll be spitting dirt all night."

Taking his friend by the hand, Jake helped him to his feet.

"Correct me if I'm wrong, but didn't I tell you I was on vacation?" Rick inquired.

Jake nodded and gave his friend a halfhearted smile. "I know, I know. You've told me a dozen times. I'm sorry. Believe me. I'm just as upset as you are, probably a damn sight more." Putting an arm around Rick, Jake helped him toward the house. It was not only bizarre but disheartening how the bones in the poor guy's body popped and cracked as they walked.

"Did you get the license number of that bus?" Rick asked.

Jake forced a grin. "Probably the same one that plowed into me." Abandoning what he knew to be real and reasonable, he whispered, "Tell me more about that nephew of yours. Leave nothing out."

Otherworldly Residents

Frustrated, tired, and shirtless, Rick leaned against the kitchen counter. Betadine covered his chest and stomach. A resolved expression plastered across his boyish face, he'd been trying to phone his nephew for what seemed hours. "*Intellectuals*. God help us. You can never reach them when they're needed."

Lindsey and Heidi sat close together at the kitchen table, the youngster sipping a glass of apple juice. It had taken a while, but she had calmed down. Physically, the six-year-old hadn't suffered a scratch. Emotionally, however, Jake suspected she had been traumatized. He had little doubt the incident on the swing set would haunt his daughter for years to come.

Standing next to Rick, Jake had both elbows bandaged and thought if his back wasn't covered with a bruise the size of a watermelon, it would be a miracle. The side effects from the stupor were still lingering and his thoughts were somewhat scattered. A fresh dose of guilt ravaged him. How was it possible he hadn't been able to help his own daughter? When he'd tried rescuing her, it wasn't as if he'd slammed into a wall. It was more as if a wall had slammed into him. Of course, he'd already come to the conclusion that whatever this thing was, it was something vicious and imperceptible. He rubbed his forehead—the beginnings of a headache were making itself known. He was doing his best to stay calm on the outside, but on the inside all hell was breaking loose. He wasn't the kind of person to take something like this lightly. Lindsey was right. They were under attack—an attack from something that wasn't showing itself. And there was no denying who the culprit was. A ghost. One of several. A ghost who sought to hurt children. A ghost who was capable of knocking two grown men to the ground. By God, just two days ago, he hadn't even *believed* in ghosts.

Rick was still on the phone, his eyes enormous, his voice deafening. "Hello, Julian? This is your Uncle Richard." He paused and rolled his eyes. "Calm down. No one died. I just need your help."

Jake turned his attention to Lindsey sitting at the kitchen table, her coffee untouched, clearly focused on their daughter.

"No," shouted an exasperated Rick. "I don't need *money*, Julian. I want you to do something for me. Something right up your alley."

It had taken all this time but finally Jake recalled Heidi screaming someone's name while she was on the swing. It was astonishing how the mind could be capable of blocking out such vital information while under stress. "Honey, who were you calling for when we were trying to get you off the swing?"

Heidi took a hearty swig of apple juice and took her time answering. Jake was familiar with his daughter's stall tactics. She was being cautious. Something else must have happened, something important, and she was doing her best to stay out of trouble.

"Yes," Rick shouted into the phone. "The *Breckinridge* Mansion, that's right. I want you to dig up everything you can on it."

A pensive Lindsey swallowed and turned to Heidi. A registered nurse, his wife could be exceptionally observant under fire. "Honey, *who's* Sarah?"

Heidi peered at her mother, a dubious expression crossing

her face. "She's someone who used to live here," she answered. "She's Vicki's mom."

"And Vicki's your friend?"

Heidi nodded.

"And Vicki and Sarah are *ghosts*?"

Again, Heidi nodded. "Sarah saved me by throwing a rock at the rattlesnake." She took a cautious breath, and Jake knew some gut-wrenching news was about to rear its ugly little head. "She also saved me from the refrigerator. I was locked inside . . . and she opened it."

Pouncing away from the counter, Jake shook with rage. "That piece of junk on the other side of the garage? Heidi, you could have suffocated! I told you not to leave the yard."

Lindsey held up her hand and gave Jake a look that told him to back off and pipe down. Taking a deep breath, she turned to their daughter. "Are Sarah and Vicki *good* ghosts, honey?"

Again, Heidi nodded.

"But there's a *bad* ghost, isn't there?"

In the background Jake heard Rick's voice loud and clear. "Yeah, meet me there tomorrow. No, in the morning, the sooner the better." Not once in the more than twenty-four years he had known Rick had Jake ever seen his friend this amped up. He'd always envied his buddy's composure. While they were in high school, he would never take any of the bullies' taunts personally. He would merely say, "I think you're right," and casually walk away. Jake, on the other hand, would explode and get into a knock-down, drag-out fight and wind up suspended from school.

"I don't care, Julian, it's going to have to be enough time," Rick concluded. Not bothering to say goodbye, he hung up.

Heidi took another swallow of apple juice before answering her mother. She was undoubtedly frightened, and Jake didn't know if she was merely afraid of getting into trouble or afraid of something else.

"Is there a bad ghost in this house?" Lindsey prompted her daughter.

"Yes, Mommy," Heidi whispered. "He's a *bad* ghost, and he

wants to hurt us." She slumped down and her face turned scarlet. "Hurt us really bad." She wiped away a tear. Jake thought his heart would never recover. "Vicki told me he wants to kill us."

Jake cringed and barely held himself together. He could almost hear the wheels turning inside of Lindsey's head. How she was able to stay calm was beyond him.

"Do you know the name of this ghost?" Lindsay asked, her voice tender and supportive.

Gazing at her drink, Heidi shrugged. "I don't know, Mommy. Vicki doesn't know either."

"Why would this ghost want to hurt us?"

Staring at her mother, Heidi's eyes filled with dread. "Because he's mean and likes to kill people."

Lindsey glanced at her husband, her eyes anxious but her spirit stronger than ever.

Jake muttered under his breath. He'd had enough. It was all he could do not to punch a wall or throw a chair across the room. He hadn't lost his temper since he was eighteen, but this was his family, his loving wife and innocent daughter. He took a massive breath, grabbed a Corona from the refrigerator, and downed it in six gulps. The hell with it still being morning. Rick was right. What in God's name had he gotten Lindsey and Heidi into?

***

It was nearly midnight and Jake knew his chances of sleeping were about the same as winning the lottery. After their conversation in the kitchen, it was decided that Heidi wasn't going to spend another night in the Breckinridge Mansion, at least not until it was safe. Cramming a suitcase full of clothing, dolls, and stuffed animals, Lindsey drove their daughter to her older sister's house in Huntington Beach. Heidi would remain there for as long as necessary.

A year older than Lindsey, Diane had proven herself to be a supportive and helpful sister, and Jake had always liked her. The downside was that Heidi might miss some school, but that was a lot better than her being suffocated, bitten by a rattlesnake, or her neck being broken on a runaway swing.

Jake tried talking Lindsey into staying with Diane as well. Of course she refused. "We're in this together," she had insisted. "If we're going to fight this thing, we're going to fight it side by side." To make matters worse, Rick refused to go home, claiming he would be needed to deal with his nephew, whatever that meant.

It took all day for Lindsey to make the drive to her sister's and back again. While she was gone, Jake and Rick loaded up the abandoned refrigerator and hauled it to the dump. After that, they worked on the sprinkler system for a couple hours. The three of them ate dinner around seven, then watched a documentary called "The Battle of the Bulge" on the History Channel. There were no further incidents concerning ghosts. Now it was late, and both Lindsey and Rick had gone to bed but Jake was still wide awake.

He tried watching television. He kept flipping channels, looking for something to get his mind off their problems. Even with the newly installed cable, every now and then the picture would cut out. He came upon an old black-and-white movie called *The Uninvited* that looked promising, but after a few minutes, he realized it was a ghost story and turned it off.

Retrieving the last beer from the refrigerator, Jake grabbed the most boring book he could find—*Moby Dick*. He read for nearly a half hour but it didn't help. His back and elbows hurt and his mind kept seeing his little girl being hurled through the air. He was emotionally drained but still wide awake. His stress level had maxed out. His regime of keeping busy, of practicing mind control and relaxation, had been thoroughly trounced by a swing and a refrigerator. In 'Nam—fighting the Cong, mosquitoes, and monsoons—all he'd had to worry about was himself. Sadly, things had changed. Now he had himself, his family, and Rick to worry about.

As their grandfather clock in the entryway chimed 1 a.m., Jake shut the double doors to his office and sat down in front of his computer. Taking a deep breath, he stroked his beard and adjusted his glasses. Perhaps a little catching up might help. He could pay a couple of bills, balance his checkbook and, with any luck, find some relief for his insomnia.

As Jake proceeded, the den lights flickered and he nearly lost what he was working on. Was there something wrong with the power? The night sky had been exceptionally clear, the wind all but nonexistent, so it wasn't interference from the atmosphere.

The lights flickered some more, then the noise began, the same sound that both he and Lindsey had heard before: a bump followed by a squeak. Repeated over and over. It wasn't coming from an upstairs bedroom this time but from downstairs.

Bump, squeak. Bump, squeak.

He could hear the sound all too well. Each time he heard it, the louder it became. Jake swallowed. It felt as if his throat had been lined with cotton. The sound was coming closer, from somewhere in the living room, making its way toward his office.

Bump, squeak. Bump, squeak.

It was now just beyond the double doors. Jake took a nervous breath and swung around in his chair. The doors were closed and the noise had stopped. Had it gone away or was it just beyond the entrance? *Too bad*, he mused. Too bad he was someone who always had to get to the bottom of things, a natural-born investigator, because he would much rather stay in his office where it was safe. But he had to know what was going on, damn it. He simply *had* to.

Jake stood and made his way to the double doors. Although his office was a large room, the doors were only about twenty feet away. Tonight, the distance felt much farther, more like a football field away.

Something is right outside those doors. What am I going to find this time? The same little old lady dusting furniture? Or the ghost who wants to kill us?

Reaching the entrance, he placed his hand on the glass door knob. His arms felt heavy and his palms were clammy. Grasping the knob, he felt a droplet of sweat trickle down his face. The temptation to kid himself grew rampant. What were the odds that he would only find either Lindsey or Rick beyond the doors? He sneered and cursed under his breath. About a million to one.

The doors creaked open. Jake's jaw dropped. His heart all but stopped. A man in his mid-eighties, wearing some type of military uniform, was laboring his way toward the living room. The old guy was transparent and missing his left leg at the knee. Under his armpit, a crude, wooden crutch assisted his progress. The elderly gent must have sensed that someone was standing behind him, because he paused, pivoted on the crutch, and turned toward Jake. The soldier wore a wide brim hat with the emblem "C.S.A." on the front. He had a bushy gray beard and thick eyebrows.

He's a Civil War veteran, Jake realized. *He probably died a century ago.*

As if he were staring at a six-foot tall maggot, the elderly Confederate regarded him with outright disgust. For Jake, it was the longest moment of his life. Then, as he watched, the man turned and plodded away.

Bump, squeak. Bump, squeak.

The bump was the old man's crutch as it struck the wooden floor, the squeak the heel of his right boot. As he hobbled off, the soldier vanished at the center of the living room. The sound, however, continued.

Bump, squeak. Bump, squeak.

Jake turned off his computer and finished his Corona before going to bed. It didn't help. It would take a lot more than beer to subdue his thoughts. For Jake McKay, there would be little sleep, or even a moment's peace, as long as he and Lindsey remained in the Breckinridge Mansion.

* * *

Rick also had a long night, only managing to doze off and on. During one of his short-lived sleeps, he dreamed he drove to Kincaid College and descended down a crumbling stone staircase to locate his nephew. Cobwebs were everywhere, hindering his progress. To his horror, Julian wore a laboratory jacket covered in blood. Like a mad scientist from a Frankenstein movie, he possessed countless bottles of bubbling potions and elaborate electronic equipment spread throughout a gigantic dungeon. At the room's center stood an enormous operating table. Lying on the table, its face concealed by a towel, Rick spotted a nearly seven-foot cadaver.

"I'm gonna bring this poor, pathetic creature back to life, Uncle Richard," roared Julian, a demented grin distorting his childish face.

Overwhelmed by a combination of fear and disgust, Rick stepped back to the far wall and observed his nephew's maniacal behavior. His frail body a mere five-feet, five-inches tall, his dark, unruly hair standing on end, and the thick lenses of his glasses cracked, Julian laughed as if he were a lunatic on a killing spree. "This wretched body will live again, Uncle Richard. It will live a long and productive life as the *greatest* scientific creation in history!"

With that Julian pulled a lever. Electrical sparks crackled from the equipment and the body convulsed. As the towel slipped from its face, Rick could only gawk in terror. With deep surgical scars running across its forehead, and metal bolts implanted on its neck, the monster appeared to be a dead ringer for Jerry Springer.

Rick shot up in bed. "Holy shit," he hollered, finding his throat devoid of moisture. It took him considerable effort to swallow. He gradually became aware of the previously still wind as it whistled through the house and of a window shutter banging against an outside wall. *Looks like the contractors missed that,* he decided. Fully alert, he gazed at the alarm clock on the nightstand. It read 3:11, the same time the woman in the negligee had appeared the night before.

Rick turned toward the rocking chair. His stomach caved and his heart jumped. Once again, there was a shadow that looked to be human within its confines—a much larger shadow this time. At first he couldn't make out the details, but steadily, his eyes adjusted.

It wasn't the woman in the negligee but a large, African-American man. Wearing a long-sleeve red shirt and what appeared to be faded jeans, he was of stocky build and kept his eyes lowered.

Leaning forward, Rick was about to speak when he discovered the intruder wasn't *sitting* on the rocking chair but was absorbed into it from the waist down.

Rick's heart rate accelerated. He couldn't believe this was happening a second time. *Another ghost, one that we haven't seen before.* A gruesome possibility crossed his mind. *Is this the ghost who's been trying to murder Lindsey and Heidi?*

His mind raced. He was wide awake, facing a man who lingered in the spirit world and who just may be preparing to kill him.

Rick leaned forward. The bed squeaked and the visitor raised his eyes. A surreal eeriness took over—as if a fast-forward switch had been activated. Rick's and the man's eyes locked together in what felt like a power struggle. Despite the darkness, the ghost's features became crystal clear. Everything inside Rick bottomed out. The intruder was a middle-aged black man with the most *piercing blue* eyes.

The expression on the man's face transformed into rage. His eyes grew hostile, driving icy shudders through every square inch of Rick's body. Horrified, he couldn't imagine a more terrifying sight.

The man rose into the air, his face seething with anger. In a distinct gesture of defiance, he raised his arm, clenched his fist into what resembled a wrecking ball, and shook it at Rick. Flying just below the ceiling, he disappeared into the wall behind the bed's headboard.

Cold, mind-numbing silence dominated the room. Rick's heart pounded without mercy, without a hint of slowing down. *Looks like I just ran into one pissed-off ghost.*

A wave of crippling loneliness devasted Rick. He didn't know why, but it felt as if he were the last person on the face of the planet. Cringing, he wiped the beads of sweat from his forehead. Out of breath, he leaned into the headboard, trying to gather his thoughts.

This latest confrontation wasn't lost on him. He was despised and unwanted, a fact that was *painfully* obvious. The look on the man's face—and *especially* his eyes—said it all.

A wary gasp escaped Rick. What about Jake and Lindsey? Rick was merely a *visitor* at the mansion. The McKays had actually moved in and were *permanent residents.* If that ghost despised a visitor, how would he feel about the new owners?

Rick would remain awake for the rest of the night, his mind conjuring image after image of the man's enraged blue eyes and balled-up fist.

Revelations

"Okay, we have the woman Sarah and her little girl, Vicki," Jake stated while sitting at a table in the college library. The room wasn't as large as most libraries, but small and intimate, with the scent of orange furniture polish throughout.

Rick paced between the table and a large, plate-glass window. "There's also the two I saw, the sexy woman—" He hesitated and cringed. "And the black man."

Jake nodded and glanced at his watch. It was just after eleven. Julian had kept them waiting for over forty-five minutes. How much longer was this going to take? Jake cleared his throat and turned toward his friend. "With the old woman and the soldier, that makes six . . . just like Mrs. Hampton claimed." He adjusted his glasses and peered across the room.

Rick's nephew sat at a table facing them, completely focused on his laptop, collecting all kinds of information on the Breckinridge Mansion. Apparently, he'd been at it off and on ever since Rick had called. Knowing that college libraries were usually closed on Sundays, Jake had asked Rick how his nephew had managed to get them inside.

"Easy," he had answered, "Julian's the head librarian and has the keys. His social life is as bad as mine and he spends his weekends working on his thesis."

Despite Julian's high IQ, Jake wasn't impressed with the so-called genius. With thick, unruly hair, black-rimmed glasses, and a loud, obnoxious voice, Julian reminded him of Jerry Lewis in the movie *The Nutty Professor*. Returning to their conversation, Jake asked his friend, "So which one of the ghosts do we have to worry about?"

"I bet it's the one I saw," Rick insisted. "The black man with the red shirt."

Still watching Julian, Jake responded, "Possibly. I think we can eliminate the woman and the little girl. They're not only harmless, they're actually helpful, especially since the woman rescued Heidi."

"I still say it's the black guy," Rick repeated. "He was *unbelievably* hostile. You should have seen his eyes. The most hateful eyes I've ever seen. He wanted to kill me. I know it."

"We can eliminate the old woman too." Jake crossed his arms and chuckled. "She was too *terrified* to be dangerous."

Rick's pacing came to a halt. "I'm telling you, Uncle Jake, it's the black guy. The way he shook his fist at me, I nearly *pissed* the bed."

"Maybe so." Jake drummed his fingers on the table, determined to consider every possibility. "But the sexy woman, she's a suspect too. The way you described her . . . she sounds . . . *aggressive*."

Rick glanced down the aisle of towering bookshelves then back at Jake. "Yeah, you're right. She seemed capable of just about anything." He straightened his shoulders and crossed his arms. "You know, I'm the one who dealt with the scary ones. You got off easy, Uncle Jake. All you ran into was a little old lady and a one-legged soldier."

"I wouldn't want to trade places with you, Uncle Rick, that's for sure. But that old soldier gave me a look the sent shudders up my spine. He wasn't exactly congenial, if you know what I mean."

"Guess it was quite the night for both of us," Rick concluded.

Jake jumped to his feet. Apparently, Julian had finished his research and was on his way over. The kid even walked funny, like he had a corncob stuck up his ass.

Rick unfolded his arms; his demeanor seemed anxious but he was in full control. "So what have you found, Julian?"

"Not so loud," the librarian scolded.

Jake's longtime friend sighed and shook his head. "Julian, there's no one else here. The library's closed, remember?"

The kid glanced around and shrugged his bony shoulders. "Oh, yeah, I forgot."

Rick reiterated, "Well, what have you got?"

Instead of answering, Julian ogled Jake through his thick, smudged glasses. "Now, who's this again?"

"This is my friend Jake McKay," Rick responded, clearly straining to remain patient. "Jake, this is my nephew, Julian Humphrey."

They shook hands, the limpest, wettest handshake Jake had ever endured, all the while the kid staring at him as if he were an oversized baboon.

"Humphrey?" asked Jake.

"Yeah, he's my sister's kid. Different last name."

Jake forced a smile, released the handshake, and suppressed the urge to wipe his palm. "Humphrey? Like in Bogart?"

A blank expression jetted across Julian's lily-white face. "Bogart? Who's that? Is he a politician or something?"

Jake's eyebrows arched. Leaning toward Rick, he whispered, "And you call this kid a historian?"

"On ghosts," Rick shot back. "Not on actors."

Oblivious, Julian flopped into a chair as Jake returned to his. The kid wore Bermuda shorts and a pinstriped, long-sleeve shirt, the pocket jammed with pens and pencils. "I didn't find out a *whole* lot," he replied, fiddling with his laptop. "Just some background stuff. Not anything earth shattering."

"Like what?" Rick pressed.

"Well, the original owner built the mansion in 1860. His name was Lieutenant Colonel Sedgwick Breckinridge, and he was born to a wealthy Virginia family in 1824." The kid wheezed as he talked. Jake suspected he was asthmatic and needed an inhaler. "He attended West Point and graduated in 1849. He was ranked eighteenth in his class. Not first rate, but not shabby, either." With his high-pitched voice, the kid even sounded like Jerry Lewis.

"You found all that out on your laptop?"

Julian nodded. "Affirmative, Uncle Jake."

Jake cringed and bit down on both lips. Something about the kid calling him "Uncle" left a queasy feeling in his stomach. Rick stepped back and covered his mouth, no doubt stifling a laugh. Jake wasn't amused.

Julian cleared his throat and continued. "As the records demonstrate, even though Colonel Breckinridge was living in California, he fought for the Confederacy, probably out of loyalty for his home state." A laugh, more like a sequence of snorts, escaped the kid. "That makes sense because of the emblem Uncle Jake saw."

"Emblem?"

"Yeah, the one on the old guy's hat: C.S.A., the Confederate States of America." Julian rolled his eyes. "Any moron knows that."

Jake sat back. "His left leg was missing at the knee," he added grimly.

Again, the kid nodded. As he talked, his glasses tended to creep down his nose. "That's right. He lost it at the battle of Petersburg. Too bad, because that was during the final days of the Civil War. Until then, he'd gone without a scratch. After the war he came home to find his wife had taken their children and run off with another man. Guess she got lonely living in that big house in the middle of nowhere."

Jake noticed that the kid's hands were empty—no hard copies of his research. He'd only met this so-called genius a little while ago and already he wanted to strangle him. "You didn't *print* any of this?"

"What for?" Julian asked, crossing his skinny legs. "I have a photographic memory and an IQ of one eighty."

Jake shook his head, his patience wavering on extinction. Now he knew why Rick had insisted on sticking around to deal with his nephew. "What else?" he prompted.

"Well, the colonel lived in the house until his death in 1901. Now, get this. At seventy-seven, he hung himself on the stairwell banister. He probably had cancer and didn't want to suffer." He took a raspy breath and sighed. "That's a horrible way to go. I think it would have been easier on him to stick a gun into his mouth. Messy but quick."

Jake and Rick exchanged glances.

"The colonel never remarried, but, and this is the interesting part, he *didn't* live alone. A former slave of his, Jacob Hancock, lived with him. For some spending money and room and board, he kept the mansion up, and over the years, they became good friends. When Colonel Breckinridge killed himself, Hancock inherited the mansion, living in it until 1914, when he died." Julian's shrill voice turned somber. "He killed himself too, but the records don't say how." Grinning broadly, Julian displayed an incredible overbite. "Jacob Hancock must have been the black man you saw, Uncle Richard. The ghost with blue eyes. One of his parents must have been white."

"No kidding," Jake muttered. "What else?"

The kid pushed his glasses back up his nose. "That's it. *Punto final.*"

"What about Sarah and the little girl?"

Julian frowned and peered at his laptop. "Without last names, I can't find them here."

"What about town records? City Hall must have something."

The kid nodded. "I can check this afternoon. Gosh, Uncle Richard, don't you think what I dug up is out of this world . . . no pun intended?"

Rick approached his nephew and shook his hand. "Of course, Julian. You did a *fantastic* job. Thank you."

"You're welcome, Uncle Richard, but I'm afraid no matter how much information I come up with, it won't get *rid* of the problem."

Rick frowned. "Yeah, you're right, Julian. What do you suggest?"

"You need a *medium*," Julian blurted. "An honest-to-goodness psychic." He glanced back and forth between the two men. "But you'd better be careful. There are a lot of phony-baloneys out there. Comes with the territory."

Bolting from his seat, Jake fumed. All this pointlessness and now the little egghead wanted them to find a medium? He gave the kid a look that would turn a baby's hair gray. "A psychic? You want us to hire a . . . *psychic*? This whole thing's getting out of hand." It took a lot for Jake to go ballistic, but just the thought of hiring some witch doctor sent him skedaddling head-first over the line.

"Yep, that's right. You need a real pro. An *actual* professional. Not some quack." The kid snorted again. "California's full of quacks. Any moron knows that."

Rick slipped his hands into his pockets. He stared at his nephew as if he were staring down the barrel of a Colt .45. "Do you know anyone, Julian?"

The librarian proudly beamed, once again displaying his overbite. "Affirmative, my illustrious uncle. In fact, she's a former professor of mine and will probably help you for nothing. The woman's a saint."

Rick placed a hand on the kid's shoulder. "Is she nearby?"

Julian's smile suddenly vaporized and a forlorn expression distorted his cartoonish face. "Yes, Uncle Richard, I know where she's at." His tone had become guarded, strangely remote. Again, he pushed his glasses back up the bridge of his nose. "I'll take you to her if you'd like."

Jake stood. "You don't sound too sure of yourself. What's wrong with her?"

Julian's expression remained unchanged. He took another raspy breath. "You'll see, but I gotta tell you, she's the best. The *absolute* best. There's no one any better. I would recommend her with my dying breath."

The corners of Jake's mouth curled upward. *That could be*

arranged, he mused.

Rick took his nephew by an elbow. "If you say so, Julian, that's all I need to hear. Come on, let's get going. We left Lindsey alone and need to get back to the mansion as fast as possible."

After the kid locked the library door, the three of them rushed into the nearly vacant parking lot. From then on, things became so hectic that Julian didn't have time to research the town hall records.

The Wind Witch

While Jake and Rick were away, Lindsey made a rush trip to the nearest strip mall, which was just south of downtown Santa Domingo. They were out of milk, bread, beer, laundry detergent and a few other items. She pulled her Camry into the Arco station and parked in front of the convenience store. Since moving in, this was her second trip to this particular location.

The elderly man at the register was the same clerk who had waited on her the time before. He was of average height, moderately overweight, with thick salt-and-pepper hair and a scraggly beard. He wore black-rimmed glasses that hung from an elastic band around his neck. The whites of his dark eyes were constantly red, the right eye wandering to the left every now and then.

"Just passing through?" the man inquired as he bagged the groceries, including a pack of Marlboro cigarettes for Jake and a liter of Diet Pepsi for Rick.

"No," she answered. "We just recently moved here from Fontana."

The man chuckled, a bitter edge to his tone. He wore a name badge that read "Murray." "Why would you want to move here of all places? It's hotter than hell in the summer, colder than a lawyer's heart in the winter, and worst of all, there's *no* work."

"Oh, we'll be commuting to work. I'm a nurse and my husband's a high school teacher."

The man nodded and grunted. "Nice. Those are good jobs." He finished bagging the items and slid the plastic bag across the counter toward her. "That'll be twenty-five dollars and fifty-three cents."

Lindsey handed him a twenty and a ten, and he pulled the change from the resister. "Did you move into the new housing tract?"

With everything that had happened in the last few days, Lindsey felt reluctant to bring up the mansion. "No, we moved into a place just outside of town."

The man froze and a look of gloom crossed his craggy face. "You don't mean the Breckinridge Mansion, do you?"

Lindsey nodded and braced herself. "Yes . . . a-are you familiar with it?" Her voice sounded childlike and anxious, even to herself.

What appeared to be an involuntary gasp escaped Murray. He stared at her for what seemed the longest time. His bloodshot eyes grew uncomfortably piercing. "Most folks around here are familiar with the place," he replied in a hushed tone, handing her the change. She couldn't shake those eyes of his. He stared at her as if she were an Ebola victim from a Third World country. "I'm not much on telling folks what to do, but if I were you, I'd pack my bags and move out. Sooner the better."

Cringing, Lindsey, picked up the bag and held it against her chest. "Why would you say that? Because it's supposed to be haunted?"

The man shrugged. "That's what I've heard. But I've never been *inside* the place. Don't want to either."

Frustrated, Lindsey shook her head and backed her way toward the exit. The bag had grown heavy and she switched it to her right hand. "Then why on earth would you—" she stammered, sighed, and then cleared her throat. "Never mind. Thanks for the suggestion."

The man eased the register shut. "I don't know about it being haunted, but there's things worse than that. My son, Frankie, was good friends with the contractors that restored the place. Two brothers, Dennis and Danny Jensen. Good boys who got along with Frankie just fine. They're dead now, both brothers, killed in separate car crashes. One drunk, the other on drugs. Frankie told me that Danny Jensen claimed he *saw* stuff in that house. So terrible he was too shook up to talk about it. Stuff that was too much for Danny, and maybe Dennis, too."

Lindsey could hardly contain herself. She shifted the plastic bag from her right hand to her left. "So your son never found out what kind of stuff?"

The old man shook his head. "No, neither of the Jensen brothers would say. But Frankie . . . he thought it was something *satanic*."

***

With the dryer out of commission, Lindsey carried the overflowing laundry basket outside. She started with the linens, hanging each item on the clothesline just behind the house. It was 11:50 and the day was warming up.

Despite knowing that their home was haunted, and coping with all the danger they'd endured, life had to go on. Someone had to take care of the chores, the everyday items. Now that Heidi was safe, Jake, who had been gone for over two hours, was doing everything he could to put an end to their problem. Besides, finally, she was keeping busy and preoccupied with something other than ghosts. She had already recovered from the incident at the convenience store. It was a beautiful, clear morning, with the nearby mountains outlined against the horizon in stunning clarity.

Retrieving the clothespins she'd found in the basement's storage cabinet, Lindsey hung up one of Jake's shirts. Using a clothesline was new to her, but like her mother used to say, "Clothes that are dried outside smell fresher."

After hanging a blouse, Lindsey turned, and feeling a cool

breeze rush across her face, looked at the garage. A woman wearing a long nightgown stood in front of it, facing her. Due to the sun's glare, it took a moment for Lindsey's eyes to fine tune, but when they had, the hair on her arms stood on end. *Good God, she's transparent!*

The woman appeared to be in her middle to late twenties, had long, flowing blonde hair, and possessed facial features radiant beyond description. Beside her stood a young girl about Heidi's age who hugged the woman at her waist, all the while concealing her face.

Lindsey felt her heart perform a flip-flop. Were they the same spirits who had saved Heidi? They had to be. "Sarah?" she whispered, barely audible. "Vicki?"

The woman stood motionless as a breeze frolicked her nightgown. Her eyes locked onto Lindsey's, revealing a most remarkable inner tranquility. She was a ghost beyond beautiful, a virtuous spirit from an unknown time and place. Lindsey's heartbeat slackened. The woman had saved Heidi. She had rescued her from the refrigerator and the rattlesnake. She meant no harm. She was on their side.

Every now and then the little girl would glance up from her mother's waist, then bury her face back to where she obviously felt more secure. The three of them stood frozen, and Lindsey was about to ask what they wanted when the woman raised her right hand and pointed toward the front yard.

"W-what are you saying?" Lindsey asked. "Do you want us to leave?"

Continuing to point, the woman remained silent.

"Is there something in the front yard you want me to see?"

Before she could answer, the woman's tranquil expression vanished. She peered toward the apple orchard as if discovering an appalling sight.

Lindsey took a breath and turned toward the orchard. There was nothing but twenty rows of perfectly aligned apple trees, as far as she could see. Upon turning back toward the garage, both the woman and girl had vanished.

Discouraged, Lindsey called for them, but only the sound of a northerly wind responded. *Of course there's no answer. If the woman could talk, she would have done so.*

But Sarah was trying to tell her something about the front yard, something she wanted her to see. A sudden cringe scurried up Lindsey's spine. Or was her pointing meant to be something sinister? A warning, perhaps? Advice to stay away? Although the little girl had spoken to Heidi, the mother could not *or* would not speak, at least for now. A question suddenly flashed in Lindsey's mind. A rather morbid question and the type that if she dwelled on it, would keep her up for weeks on end: what in God's name could possibly scare a ghost?

Much to Lindsey's chagrin, she was still clutching a pair of clothespins, her right palm turning beet red from the pressure. Tossing the pins into the laundry basket, she approached the front yard.

***

Wiping her brow, Lindsey placed her hands on her hips. Other than the SOLD sign, the willow tree, and the PVC pipes Jake had left along the sprinkler trenches, she found nothing of interest in the front yard. With her eyes locked on the ground, she had gone over every inch of the area, all the way to the raggedy highway in front of their home and back again. There were some rusty nails, a handful of cigarette butts, a beer can, literally thousands of rocks, and even a dead lizard, but nothing significant. What was Sarah trying to tell her? Could it be about the thing that had attacked her and Heidi?

Barely audible over the breeze, something rustled behind Lindsey. Instantly, her instincts jumped to high alert. She held her breath, turned, and caught a glimpse of a shadowy, shapeless figure across the highway. Roughly a foot in diameter, it remained close to the ground, stirring a cloud of dirt into the air. The figure blended into the cloud, becoming virtually imperceptible as dead shrubs were torn from their roots and swept into its vortex.

Not more than ten feet away, a fascinated Lindsey watched

as the cloud grew into a mini tornado, or "dust devil" as her parents had called them. It whirled violently, swaying in an almost hypnotic manner, hurling stones into the air, the sound of it angry and threatening. When the dirt, dust, and debris settled to the ground, the result of the uprooted shrubs emerged before her.

Otherwise known as a wind witch, a tumbleweed five feet in diameter swayed about then started toward her. Caught off guard, Lindsey found herself unable to react. As it neared, it snagged on a shrub to the right of the willow, which held it in place.

A moment of intense surrealism followed. The sun scorched Lindsey's face. The wind whipped her back. The urge to laugh and scream besieged her. The sight of the enormous weed, nearly touching-distance away, made her feel as if they were locked into some type of inexplicable standoff.

Lindsey's thoughts scattered into fragments. The way it had rushed toward her, then stalled, it seemed obvious that it was going to attack her. *It's a tumbleweed. There's nothing to worry about. Get going. I have things to do . . .*

Her throat dried out. Her hands quivered. Again, she reminded herself that it was just a weed, gigantic in size, but a weed just the same.

Lindsey turned and proceeded toward the front porch then halted. Was it a mistake to turn her back on it? In the wake of all the bizarreness that had happened since they had moved in, she had grown overconfident, perhaps even arrogant.

Suddenly, something seized her by the wrist. She jumped and her heart nearly exploded. An abrasive strand had grabbed her—a vine that had clearly sprouted from the wind witch. Twisting and turning against her skin, it dug in hard, drawing blood and pain.

Lindsey turned and peered at the weed. It had grown considerably and was now at least six feet in diameter, towering over her like a shapeless giant as it struggled to free itself from the shrub. She fought back—twisting and turning her wrist, causing even more pain—then striking the strand as hard as she could with her free hand. After several blows, the connection snapped and she backed away.

For the longest while, Lindsey couldn't take her eyes from the thing before her. She didn't know what it was. It wasn't just a weed—something had taken control of it. The shadowy figure. Her lungs couldn't get enough air and her heart ached. Shading her eyes, she peered at the willow tree. Tumbleweeds moved with the wind. She cringed and clenched her fists. The breeze that stirred the willow rose from the opposite direction in the canyon, an *easterly* wind. The tumbleweed had rolled *against* it.

Lindsey's stomach plunged. Turning on her heels, she fled toward the house. Before that thing tore itself loose, she had to get inside. She hurried onto the front porch and grabbed the door knob. It wouldn't budge. Damn her compulsiveness! She'd always kept the front door locked, even when everyone was home. Turning toward the highway, she couldn't believe what she saw . . . or *didn't* see. The weed had vanished. *Where did it go?* She scanned the front yard. Nothing. It was as if it had never been there. *Better get going. It has to be around here somewhere.*

Swallowing, Lindsey took a frantic breath and rushed along the porch on the left side of the house, toward the door to Jake's office. Grasping the door knob, her panic escalated. Locked! God, how she *hated* herself.

Struggling over the porch railing, Lindsey kept a constant vigilance over her shoulder, her fears and vulnerability intensifying. The instant she was over, she bolted for the kitchen door at the rear of the mansion. An old hamstring injury drove sharp, little daggers into her right calf. She cringed, clutched her leg, and fought off the pain. Cursing, she pushed on. *I'm almost there. Keep moving.*

The wind blew Lindsey's hair into her face. She couldn't see. She could barely breathe. Rounding the rear corner, she skidded on a patch of gravel and, falling forward, struck her forehead on the ground. The house, the porch, the back door—everything turned into a black abyss.

***

When Lindsey regained consciousness, she was lying face down on the ground, twelve feet from the back porch. A substantial knot had formed on her forehead and throbbed when she touched it. *Oh, God! How long was I out?*

Recalling the weed, an additional round of fear tore through her. She whirled around. The wind was still rustling the apple trees, but the wind witch was nowhere to be seen. It had disappeared like an unwanted memory. As she sat up, her blood turned to ice. *What if it's still nearby?*

Suddenly, getting inside the house seemed crucial. Struggling, Lindsey rose onto unsteady legs. Her head spun. After treating head injures for fourteen years as a trauma nurse, she knew she had suffered a concussion. She gathered her strength and pushed herself, her progress slow and painful. She climbed onto the porch as if she were making her way through a dream. Reality lurked just beyond her grasp. With her movements awkward and wobbly, she opened the back door and stepped inside.

The kitchen appeared blurry and distorted, no doubt effects from her concussion. Slamming the door, she locked the deadbolt and stumbled to the kitchen sink, the knot on her forehead pounding all the while. Fighting to catch her breath, she snatched a glass from the counter and turned on the cold-water tap. Thank God! No blood gushed out this time.

Lindsey drank her fill, set the glass down, and eased into a kitchen chair. She had to regroup before putting ice on her forehead. She peered around the room, trying to comprehend what had just happened. Like some type of puppet, something must have manipulated the tumbleweed—something undoubtedly supernatural—probably the same entity that had attacked her and Heidi.

An icy chill passed through Lindsey, followed by an explosion of sound. Flinching, she braced herself. Precious moments crept by before she realized what had happened. All around her, the kitchen cabinets had flung open on their own—both above and below the counters—the pantry, the drawers, even the breadboard had been pulled out.

A prolonged quiet followed. Sitting at the table in the stillness, her nerves on edge, Lindsey listened to the frenetic pounding of her heart. *Something's in here with me. Something that wants to attack me.*

Slowly, cautiously, she rose to her feet. A keen awareness gnawed at her stomach. Staring at the cabinets to the right, she stepped toward them.

A glass shot from the cabinet. Sailing through the air, it missed Lindsey by inches. It shattered on the opposite wall, raining dozens of fragments on the floor. A second glass soared from the cabinet. Covering her head with her arms, she ducked, and it also burst against the wall behind her.

Time raced. A coffee mug broke through the gap between Lindsey's arms and struck her on the jaw, sending pain through her face. A frying pan slammed into her elbow, followed by a bowl that hit her left shoulder.

Lindsey's reflexes took over. She dropped to the floor, the broken glass cutting both her bare knees. No matter what action she took, nothing seemed to help. A second pan flew at her at a sharp angle, hitting the side of her head. Dizziness overwhelmed her. She screamed. Only her determination kept her from passing out.

More items struck, hitting Lindsey's arms, chest, and back. She crawled through the broken glass, scooted under the table, and covered herself in a fetal position. More items took flight: dishes, glasses, pots, pans, even silverware. Each item shot across the room at an incredible speed. No matter where they struck— her back, arms, or legs—the pain intensified. But somehow, she managed to protect her head. Another concussion could very well kill her.

Knowing she was unable to reach either the swinging door or the door to the back yard without serious injury, desperation overcame Lindsey. She was still taking a horrendous beating, and hiding under the table wasn't enough protection. She had to remove her arms and hands from covering her head and turn the table onto its side. She hated the idea of exposing herself, but with the table overturned, the kitchen items wouldn't be able to reach her.

Lindsey waited for a lull. Just a brief reprieve, not more than a few seconds would be enough. A fork pierced her hand. A bowl grazed her ear. Again, she fought back pain. She kept praying for a lull. She couldn't take much more. There was too much pain. Too much trauma. Damn it, was it ever going to stop, even for an instant? She had to overturn the table before the knives struck.

Katherine Price

Safe Haven Hospital

Still dressed in her terrycloth bathrobe well into the afternoon, Professor Katherine Price sat on a wicker chair, facing a window featuring a dreary view of the hospital parking lot. She scrutinized her reflection in the window. She'd always been told how beautiful she was, with her blonde hair, green eyes, flawless skin, and upturned nose. Times had changed. She could no longer see her beauty. She'd grown ugly, despondent, and useless. In her hand she held a scrap of aluminum. Last night during dinner she had managed to tear the scrap from a Pepsi can but, conflicted about killing herself, decided to wait before using it. She had even slept with it neatly tucked under her pillow.

Glancing at her watch, a beloved present from her father, Katherine fought back tears. How strange that her dad—a college professor as well—had taken his life. Perhaps suicides ran in families, a hypothesis of hers that vindicated the most self-destructive temperament. Simply stated: suicidal tendencies were the symptoms of a clandestine disease. *Genes* were the culprits—the actual insidious perpetrators—not the innocents who so helplessly succumbed to their lethal embrace.

The view of the parking lot appeared to sway ever so slightly. It would be the last thing she would ever see. Holding the scrap of aluminum between her thumb and index finger, Katherine raised it above her left wrist. Trembling, she wrestled with a lifetime of heartache. Taking her life had become her best alternative, the preferable means to an end. Suicide was a logical escape, an escape from life's pain and endless bouts of depression.

Inhaling, Katherine pressed the metal scrap into her wrist. There were so many regrets, the loss of her mother and father and her own agonizing divorce among them. She would not miss her life. Not in the least.

From the vast depths of her consciousness, a "vision" erupted. One that was dramatic and formidable. As if flipping through the pages of a photo album, countless images raced across her mind. Images of a three-story mansion with a large porch and a white and red sign in the front yard. Of a weeping willow tree and an apple orchard. A little girl materialized, then a man with a beard and glasses, a woman with long brown hair, and a second man with thick blond hair. They needed her help, clearly evident by the clarity of the vision. Something was wrong, and at this very moment, the woman was in danger. Immediate danger. The images began slowing. The woman was in the front yard, searching, but Katherine couldn't lock on to what she searched for. And there was more . . . so much more. Something unseen, cold, cruel, and calculating stalked them.

Katherine tried focusing on the outcome. Would the woman survive? Would any of them survive? With her head throbbing, she struggled to envision the future, a painful and challenging task as she battled to keep from passing out. Pushing back the dawn would have been easier. The answers proved indistinct, but before the vision faded, she found what she needed to know.

Exhaustion set in. Ever since being committed to the hospital, her energy level had deteriorated. Coping with a vision— especially one this powerful, this *extremely* overwhelming—would drain what little vitality she possessed.

An urgent knock on her door startled Katherine. Immediately, her abilities took over, revealing that it was her psychiatrist, along with a young man who was seeking her help. She closed her eyes and inhaled deeply. This visit of theirs . . . it was related directly to her vision. It wasn't the first time she had encountered such an event just prior to a plea for help. Was there time for a final good deed? Perhaps. Collecting herself, Katherine murmured, "Come in," and slipped the scrap of aluminum into her bathrobe pocket. It would keep for now. She could always use it later.

***

Accompanied by Rick and Julian, Jake sat on a couch in the hospital's visitor's lounge, rubbing his eyes. He couldn't believe his mental and physical state of mind. The same horrific scenarios kept playing over and over in his head: his failure to save Heidi from the swing and his feelings of guilt when Lindsey had been drenched with chemicals. Now, on top of everything else, he was sitting in the middle of a fancy psychiatric facility in Pomona, spinning his wheels.

At first Jake had hoped Professor Price might be one of the staff or an advisor of some kind. What a joke. He wanted to laugh out loud. What a college professor would be doing working in a mental hospital, he had no idea. No wonder Julian had such a guarded expression on his face when he was asked if the woman was nearby.

After an agonizing twenty minutes, the door to the visitor's room swung open and in came a female who had to be Katherine Price, escorted by a heavyset man in a business suit, most likely her psychologist or maybe an administrator. Jake shot to his feet; his jaw dropped. Both Rick, who had been pacing, and Julian, who had been engrossed with his laptop, appeared as if they had been taken by surprise.

Dressed in a white terrycloth bathrobe belted at the waist, Professor Katherine Price wore brown paper slippers, not exactly a good sign at a psychiatric facility. Her shoulder-length blonde hair was pulled into a ponytail. Although she wore no makeup, she appeared attractive in a sort of statuesque kind of way, with prominent cheekbones and large, piercing eyes of a very dark shade of green.

Julian stood and slinked over to her in a submissive manner. She appeared to be at least three inches taller than him, despite wearing paper slippers. Julian took Katherine's hand and greeted her in an overly cheery voice, along with moving his free hand around. "Hi, professor. Do you remember me? I'm Julian Humphrey."

Jake cringed and his stomach plunged. *Oh, terrific! This is getting better all the time. The little Einstein's using sign language.*

"I attended two of your parapsychology classes and a psych seminar at Gladstone University," the kid continued. "You autographed your book, *Malevolent Spirits*, for me."

Staring at Julian in a rather guarded manner, then at Jake, and finally at Rick, the woman nodded. Jake had to force himself not to climb the walls. Katherine didn't look anything like a college professor. Although he had practically no ability at guessing a woman's age, she was probably in her mid-thirties and could pass for one of those high-fashion models who sauntered around as if they wanted to gouge someone's eyes out.

The man who had accompanied Katherine proceeded to shake their hands, introducing himself as Doctor Lubao, her psychiatrist.

"Why don't we sit down?" Rick suggested.

As they sat, creases formed on the woman's forehead. Her expression altered from guarded to suspicious.

Great, Jake mused. He was quite familiar with psychiatric patients, having volunteered as an aide for seven months after he had graduated from high school. *She's probably paranoid. And paper slippers? She's gotta be on a suicide watch. If that's the case, I'll be damned if I'm gonna let her into my house.*

"It's been a while. I'm afraid I'm a little rusty," the librarian stated, using his hands to sign.

As Julian interpreted, Katherine signed, "That's okay, I can read lips, remember?"

"Oh, yeah," Julian responded. "I forgot."

Jake jumped up from the couch. "You didn't tell us about her not being able to talk or hear."

Julian scratched his head. He could barely get his fingertips through his thick hair. "Oh, did I leave that out? I must be absentminded."

Rick stood, took his friend by the arm, and led him to a far corner. "Let's give her a chance, Uncle Jake. What've we got to lose?"

Jake resisted the urge to shout that there was *plenty* to lose. The woman couldn't talk or hear and she was in a mental institution, for crying out loud. How could she *possibly* help them? It seemed to him that she was the one who needed help. He wanted to add that if she turned out to be the *wrong* person, or if she screwed up, someone could get hurt or killed. But as Jake peered into Rick's eyes, he realized his friend was right. Bottom line, they needed help, there was no denying that, and for now, there was no one else to turn to. Gritting his teeth, Jake nodded and returned to the couch, feeling like a beaten dog.

Julian cleared his throat and focused his attention on his former teacher. "Professor Price, we're here because we need your assistance."

As Julian interpreted, Katherine signed, "I know."

Tilting his head to the left, Julian appeared dumbfounded. "Professor," the kid continued. "I take it, then . . . that you know *why* we're here."

She signed and Julian translated, "Of course."

Fidgeting on the couch, Jake rolled his eyes. She was supposed to be a paranormal expert, not a mind reader. She'd better not get into Julian's brain. Chances were it would be a major disaster in there.

"Will you help us?" the kid asked.

Crossing her legs, Katherine stared at her former pupil for the longest time.

To Jake, she didn't appear to be as suspicious as before. Here she was in a mental hospital, but interestingly enough, she retained a respectable air about her.

Finally, Katherine signed, "I'll try."

Rick turned to Doctor Lubao. "How soon can Professor Price be discharged? Is today too soon?"

"Today would be fine," the doctor answered agreeably. "Since all charges have been dropped, Katherine's free to go." He glanced at the professor then at Rick. "As long as she agrees to six months of outpatient therapy."

Jake leaned forward, his left eyelid involuntary twitching. "C-charges? W-what charges?"

As if he had just been caught with his zipper down, the doctor turned scarlet. "You didn't know?" He peered at Katherine, who nodded without the slightest change in her now nearly—but not quite—neutral expression.

She would make one hell of a poker player, Jake decided.

"Well, Professor Price was initially committed to Safe Haven for trying to stab her boyfriend," explained Doctor Lubao.

"Wonderful!" moaned Jake, his decision regarding the bottom line taking a precarious hit. "Attempted murder. Is that all?"

Appearing uncomfortable, the doctor forced a bland smile. "But the charges were dropped some time ago, and now Katherine's a *voluntary* patient."

Jake lunged to his feet, warning lights blazing away in his head. Making his way to the same far corner as before, he waved Rick over. The distance didn't matter. Katherine was quite proficient at reading lips.

"This woman's a psycho," whispered Jake. "A sick puppy. She needs more help than we do."

Rick shook his head. "I don't see either of us coming up with a better solution. We're dealing with something supernatural here, something we don't understand. So maybe it takes someone this . . . *eccentric* . . . to deal with our problem."

Jake folded his arms and swayed on his heels, a tendency of his whenever his nerves were taking a rollercoaster ride. "She's trouble. I'd bet my life on it."

Rick nodded. "Yeah, maybe." He paused and winked. "She's smart, attractive, and wants to help. What could go wrong?"

"W-what did you say?"

Patting his friend's shoulder, Rick replied, "Calm down, Uncle Jake. I don't think we have much of a choice." As a sullen Jake watched in silence, Rick approached the seated Katherine. "Professor Price, we'd be honored if you would look into our situation."

"Katherine," she signed as Julian interpreted. "Call me Katherine."

Rick smiled and nodded. "Okay, Katherine it is. You can call me Rick or Richard, whatever you prefer." He held out his hand. "Will you help us?"

***

Professor Price stared at Rick's hand for a fleeting but intense moment. He meant no harm. He just wanted to shake in agreement, that was all. It was a simple enough gesture, yet she found herself hesitating. Why? Had she become so paranoid that she couldn't respond to a handshake? All she had to do was to take her hand out of her pocket and shake the man's hand. But something inside her wanted to hold back and not touch him, and her instincts were never unfounded. But if she didn't take his hand, she would never know why she hesitated.

Releasing the scrap of aluminum in her pocket, Katherine accepted the gesture. Like a bolt of lightning, another vision flashed through her, just as powerful as the previous one. For that brief instant, she observed this man and herself in bed together, naked, in a sweltering embrace. They would become lovers, passionate and uninhibited. She grew faint. She had to catch her breath. Now she knew why she had hesitated. But how could this possibly be, especially since she was preparing to end her life?

Aware only of the excitement of the moment, Rick turned to the psychiatrist. "Start the paperwork, Doctor Lubao," he proclaimed. "Katherine's coming with us."

***

Roaring through the pass on the interstate, Jake ground out his cigarette in the Explorer's ashtray. He couldn't believe it. For the last three years his vehicle had never given him a minute of grief. Now, of all days, it had overheated in the canyon. He glanced at his watch. It was nearly four o'clock. The incident had set them back *another* two hours.

From the moment they'd met Katherine, Jake's frustration had been building. First, there was the mountain of paperwork to get her discharged. When they were finally ready, she insisted on a late lunch. That killed another forty-five minutes. Then, as they were leaving, she wanted to stop by her apartment. There Lindsey was, by herself with all kinds of ghosts haunting the mansion, and Katherine chose to take a *shower*.

"Besides," she had explained in sign language, "I need to pick up something." It was an item, she had claimed, that would help their situation.

During lunch, a frustrated Jake had excused himself and called Lindsey from his cell phone. "Are you okay?" he had asked.

"Just hurry," was all she would say. Her voice sounded shaky. Something had happened.

When Katherine insisted on going home first and Jake balked, Julian suggested that Jake and Rick to go ahead without them. He could take Katherine home in his Volvo, then drive to the mansion when she was ready.

Jake had agreed, but thanks to a faulty thermostat, had lost an additional two hours. Having driven most of the way in silence, Jake finally looked at his friend, who appeared preoccupied. "You don't have to stay, old buddy. I know you were planning on leaving today."

Rick shook his head. "There's no hurry, Uncle Jake. I'm on vacation, remember?" He chuckled. "Besides, I'd like to see how everything turns out."

"Do you really think this woman can help?"

Rick nodded. "If my nephew thinks so, then I *know* she can."

"I hope you're right," Jake replied. "We never told her what the problem was. And she never asked. Unless Julian informs her while they're at her apartment—"

"If she's an *authentic* clairvoyant," Rick interjected. "She already knows."

Still concerned about Lindsey, Jake raced toward Exit 17, old Highway 113. They would reach their destination in five minutes. All he could think about was his wife being alone in that house all day. Sure, she had insisted, but when was he ever going to learn to put his foot down?

Pulling into the gravel driveway, Jake gawked at Julian's beat-up Volvo. As badly as he had wanted to rush home, Julian and Katherine, who had taken their time, had still managed to arrive first. It was the tortoise-and-the-hare scenario all over again.

Jake jumped out of the Explorer and spotted Lindsey waiting for him on the front porch. As he hurried toward her, it felt as if a punch came out of nowhere and smacked him square in the head. His wife looked like she had fought at the Alamo, on the losing side. There were dark circles beneath her eyes and a numb expression on her face. Along with some swelling across her jawline, and a red knot on her forehead, there was an abrasion on her right wrist plus a Band-Aid on the back of her left hand. What looked like Betadine covered her knees.

Rushing up the porch steps, Jake gave his wife a careful hug. Her arms hung limp at her sides. She displayed no tears or even the slightest bit of emotion. In fact, Lindsey seemed to be in a state of shock. "Honey, I'm sorry," he muttered. "The Explorer overheated in the middle of the interstate. Are you okay?"

Rick joined them before she could respond. "Geez, Lindsey. What happened?"

Lindsey pulled away from her husband. Jake spotted more injuries, at least three bruises on her arms. "I have something to show you," she murmured and led them through the living room, the dining room, and through the kitchen's swinging door.

In the middle of the room, the kitchen table had been overturned. To Jake's vexation, as he circled the table, he spotted the knives. Practically every kitchen knife, including two freshly sharpened butcher knives and eight steak knives, were embedded in the table's top. Additionally, the floor was covered from one end to the other with broken glass. Various pots and pans, many of them dented, were scattered about. Every kitchen cabinet and drawer stood open. The room was an all-out disaster area, like something from the eleven o'clock news.

"I left everything so you could see," Lindsey stated, her voice low. Except for the marks and bruises on her jaw, forehead, and arms, her color looked anemic.

The pit of Jake's stomach sizzled. First, he hadn't been able to save Heidi from the swing, now this. Never before had he felt so helpless. "Lindsey, I'm sorry."

"It's not your fault, Jake," she answered in a detached tone. Considering the bruise on her forehead, he thought she may have suffered a concussion. "You couldn't have done anything about it . . . except get hurt . . . or killed."

Taking off his glasses, Jake rubbed his forehead. "This whole thing is getting out of control," he whispered, his heart aching. "What the hell was I thinking when we moved here?"

Julian was meandering around the kitchen. Thoroughly engrossed in his calculator, and tapping the keys every few seconds, he appeared oblivious to the debris. A woman stood in front of the kitchen sink with her back toward them, staring out the window, probably at the swing set. She was well dressed in a white, long-sleeved, satin blouse, black skirt, and dark nylons. Under her arm was a narrow box, maroon in color, and at her feet stood a small overnight bag. At first Jake wasn't sure who this woman was. Then he concluded it had to be Katherine, and the maroon box was probably what she had wanted from her apartment.

Jake and Rick turned the table upright. Jake couldn't believe how deeply the knives had been embedded. "You could have been killed, Lindsey."

Julian then glanced up from his calculator. "Given the depth of penetration, those knives were traveling at least ninety miles an hour."

Jake felt his temples throb. First the left, then the right. He found himself wishing his head would explode and get it over with. "That does it, Lindsey. I want you to join Heidi at your sister's. It's not safe here. I won't let you stay."

Shaking her head, Lindsey folded her arms across her chest. "I'm staying. That's final. End of discussion."

Jake knew that tone. There would be no convincing her. She would remain for as long as it took to resolve their dilemma.

Rick removed one of the knives from the tabletop and inspected it. "So what do we do now?"

After a moment of silence, the woman facing the window turned around. As she did, Jake gasped. It was indeed Katherine Price, but she looked *different*. It wasn't the clothes, or make-up, or that her hair was no longer in a ponytail. And it wasn't because she'd transformed from merely attractive to radiant. It was her body language. She displayed an air of confidence that hadn't been there before. Although she seemed to have retained a certain amount of respectability at the hospital, she had still looked guarded and suspicious. Now, at this juncture, Katherine Price's appearance left no doubt that she was in her element—that she was in charge.

Stepping over, Katherine touched one of the steak knives embedded in the table. She held her fingers on the handle for a lengthy moment, then moved to the nearby cabinet. She placed her hand on the lower right-hand corner and held it there, the expression on her face neutral.

After a long, perplexing moment, Jake was rendered a shock that *actually* rivaled his encounter with the old Confederate ghost. In a slow, clear, and concise manner, Katherine *verbally* answered Rick's question. "Take me through the house. I want to see every room."

Stunned, Rick turned to his nephew. "Why didn't you tell us she could talk?"

With his upper lip curled as if he was going to sneeze, Julian murmured, "I-I didn't know. She never told me."

Katherine peered at each of them but regarded Rick the

longest. "Well, am I going to see the house or not?"

Jake cleared his throat and gestured toward the kitchen door. "Right this way, Professor." Bestowing Julian a sullen look, he added, "And you, too, Gilligan." Following them with a forlorn expression seeping into his eyes, he added, "And leave all hope behind."

***

Starting with the upstairs bedrooms, Jake, Lindsey, and Rick gave Katherine and Julian a tour of the mansion. Or more accurately, Katherine led the four of *them* through the house. With the maroon-colored box kept snugly under her arm, she stood in the master bedroom for quite some time. Drawing back the drapes in Heidi's room, she peered at the swing set. Something about it clearly fascinated her. She made her way through the other rooms on the second floor, studied the rocking chair in Rick's room, then descended the staircase and stepped into the living room. She paused in front of the fireplace, stared at each of the gargoyles, then inched toward the window. She pushed back the miniblinds, then gazed at the weeping willow tree for nearly a minute.

After that, they entered Jake's office, the dining room, and concluded in the basement. Katherine stepped inside the darkroom, peered from the ceiling to the floor, then crossed her arms and frowned. She asked no questions and made no comments. Although none of them had mentioned it, she asked to see the photograph, "The one with the blur."

Everything inside Jake came alive with equal mixtures of shock, hope, and disbelief. Had Julian told her about the photo? Or had her *abilities* informed her? If that were the case, then it looked like they had made the right choice.

With an expression of surprise flashing across her face, Lindsey hurried off to the kitchen and, shortly later, returned with the photo.

Rick pulled his nephew aside and whispered, "Did you tell Katherine about the picture?"

His eyes glued on his former professor, Julian mumbled, "No, not a word. I swear."

"How about the house? Did you tell her anything about this house?"

Julian shook his head. "No, Uncle Richard. Except for mentioning you had some paranormal problems, I told her nothing." He shrugged. "She never even asked."

After examining the photo, Katherine handed it back to Lindsey. Taking a heavy breath, she suggested they return to the dining room.

"Of course," Jake and Lindsey replied in unison.

Suspecting Katherine had decided to get down to business, a skeptical Jake led the way. A sense of impending doom crept into his every pore. As it turned out, ghosts were as real as politicians, pedophiles, and jury duty, and they were capable of hurting or even killing people, which they had found out the *hard* way. But clairvoyants, psychics, or whatever you wanted to call them were another matter. Katherine would just have to prove herself, not an easy task even if she was the real McCoy. But Jake had to admit, so far she had been right on track. Nevertheless, his guts were in constant turmoil, telling him everyone was in for a rough ride. A humdinger, to put it mildly.

The In-Between

Katherine sat at the head of the dining room table. Except for the occasional curious glance at Rick, she appeared calm and elegant. When she situated the maroon box in front of her, Jake discovered its identity. What she *vehemently* had to retrieve from her apartment—what she couldn't do without—was, of all things, a Scrabble game. From the condition of the box, the contents had to be forty or fifty years old.

To Jake, the appearance of the game seemed melodramatic, something along the lines of—how Julian had put it—what a *charlatan* would bring. Falling back into his skeptical mode, Jake shook his head and flopped into the chair at the far end of the dining room table, keeping distance between himself and Katherine. *Great, a Scrabble game. What are we going to do now? Play parlor games?*

Katherine removed the playing board from the box, set it on the floor beside her, then dumped the tiles out. She moved with all the finesse of a veteran blackjack dealer. She spread the tiles across the table in front of her, making sure the letters were facing up.

Jake rolled his eyes but remained determined to keep his

mouth shut. Lindsey had nicknamed him "Eeyore," after the donkey in the Winnie-the-Pooh books, because of his negative tendencies. In this particular situation, however, he deserved a break. To Jake McKay, some good old-fashioned pessimism seemed the only way to go. Because they had been so blatantly desperate, they ended up recruiting a woman with a history of violence. As he waited at the table, biting his tongue and holding back a tidal wave of negativity, his worst fears bubbled to the surface: that this effort would prove to be a colossal disaster and a pathetic waste of time. Everything seemed to be slowly but surely unraveling, and they were now literally spinning their wheels with a former mental patient.

Lindsey, Rick, and Julian joined them at the table. Lindsey sat next to Jake on his left. Holding his laptop, Julian sat next to Jake on his right. Rick sat between his nephew and Katherine. With the Scrabble tiles in order, Katherine announced she was ready. She placed both her hands on the table, roughly twelve inches from the tiles. Inhaling deeply, she closed her eyes.

Now what? Jake wondered, doing his utmost to keep what was left of his patience from crumbling. Were they going to hold hands and chant? He would be damned if he was going to hold Julian's clammy paw.

Katherine made no such demands. In her slow and deliberate manner, she murmured, "I would like to speak to Sarah. Are you near, Sarah? Can you hear me?"

Except for the unusually loud ticking of their pendulum clock that sat on the cupboard behind Jake, and the occasional outside breeze, the room remained hushed. His mind wandered. *It'll be cooler tomorrow*, he suspected. The wind through the mountain pass meant fairer weather, at least that's what he'd been told. He glanced at his watch. It was already after 5:30 and growing dark.

Katherine repeated the question. "Are you there, Sarah?"

As if they had a life of their own, three of the tiles moved forward. They made their way through the other tiles and slowly inched toward Katherine. It was a sight that sent a shudder down Jake's spine. A sight he would have never imagined, not for a second. The letters came together side by side in front of the professor. They spelled YES.

Wrinkling his brow, Jake sat back. *How the hell did she do that? Some kind of illusion? Or am I just being too hard on her?*

Katherine opened her eyes and, peering at the letters, asked, "Can you help us?"

After a lengthy moment, the Y and S tiles moved away from the center E tile, then halted and slowly moved back together. Once again they spelled YES.

A hint of anticipation seeped into Katherine's voice. Swallowing she inquired, "Are Jake and Lindsey McKay in danger?"

Immediately, the three letters split apart, and once again came together. The answer remained YES.

It had grown so quiet that Jake thought their pendulum clock had stopped. While everyone watched, Katherine placed the palm of her right hand on top of the three tiles and held it there. Jake shifted in his chair. *Now what is she doing?*

Katherine's eyes, normally a piercing green, went blank, then closed. She remained motionless, so much so that Jake could have sworn she had stopped breathing.

A much more attentive Jake peered at Lindsey. Maybe she had an idea what was going on. His wife, appearing pale and anxious, glanced back and shrugged her shoulders. Evidently, Katherine had gone into some kind of trance, a type of hypnotic state where they weren't supposed to disturb her. That was Jake's best guess, since seances—or whatever this was—didn't come with an instruction manual. So now they had to sit and wait. He hated waiting. Supermarket lines, street signals, all of it. It seemed as if he'd spent half his life waiting.

What Jake didn't know was how dark and frightening a place Katherine had gone into.

***

Katherine inched through a fog that clung to the ground as if it were nipping at her ankles. The ominous world between life and the hereafter had always been engulfed in gloom and bleakness. Although she had left her body behind in the world of the living, and allowed the essences of herself to take control, a damp cold still made itself known. Of the dozens of times she had entered this world—what she referred to as the *In-Between*—never before had it been so frigid.

Wrapping her arms around herself, Katherine inched forward. She was outdoors but had no idea of her whereabouts. She could be within the In-Between's version of Europe, America, Asia, or anywhere. It was twilight. It was always twilight in the land of the In-Between, never daylight or nighttime. The fog climbed higher and grew thicker. Several objects drifted through the air in a rather graceful, leisurely manner, historical artifacts from the immediate area: a hangman's noose, a silver dollar, a razor blade. A crop of apple trees emerged. Halting, she turned to her left and stared at great length. A towering three-story structure appeared before her and quickly materialized into the Breckinridge Mansion. She had transported to the In-Between's version of the McKays' property, all of it inhabited by the souls of the dead, either lost or refusing to move on.

As if she had just entered a turbulent wind tunnel, new images whirled around her. They appeared so quickly she could scarcely make them out: calendar pages swirling through the fog; the apples in the nearby orchard rotting on their branches; eyes the color of blood, glaring at her from behind thorny shrubs. Something felt terribly wrong. Never before had the In-Between felt so dreadful. A vile presence had taken control.

Suddenly, the terrible sensations dissipated. A young, beautiful woman wearing a long, flowing nightgown emerged. Katherine sensed that this was Sarah. At her side, wearing a frilly dress, stood a little girl. Appearing to be about six-years-old, she seemed *deathly* afraid as she kept an anxious watch over her shoulder.

Sarah spoke *directly* to Katherine. As in all of her visions, and in all her excursions to the In-Between, she didn't have to read lips. She always heard perfectly. The woman talked so fast, however, that her words were hard to catch. Someone, she insisted, was "too powerful," and "the McKays should leave before it was too late." The mansion "wasn't safe" and the most predominant warning: that "their lives are at risk."

Other information flooded in about Sarah and the little girl. Katherine had always referred to this type of phenomena as "psychic energy," knowledge that came to her from interacting with a spirit. Depending upon the source, the knowledge varied in both quality and quantity. Sarah, it seemed, was highly motivated and forthright.

Then Sarah and the child disappeared, and Katherine found herself standing in a dimly lit bedroom that she wasn't familiar with but knew it was one of the mansion's five bedrooms. She glanced around. There was a bed, nightstand, and dresser. The window drapes to her left billowed in a chilly breeze. Katherine wasn't surprised that the window was closed but the fog still swirled about her. Such occurrences were commonplace in the world of the In-Between.

Instinctively, she approached the mirror. Within its boundaries an elderly woman materialized. Dressed in a powder-blue bathrobe, the woman appeared dismayed. Her name was Abigail McClellan, a spinster, the last survivor of a wealthy family. Her psychic energy kept pouring in, and it took the professor a moment to pinpoint what troubled her. In the back of Katherine's mind, she distinguished chattering that was feeble and frantic. To Abigail the house was in complete disarray. The contents of several boxes hadn't been put away and the furniture was much too dusty. Everything had to be neat. Everything had to be tidy.

Abigail vanished and Katherine found herself standing in the middle of Jake's office, but it wasn't his office, not for many years to come. Built-in bookshelves surrounded her. A rolltop desk appeared at a far corner. A kerosine lamp burned dimly on a wooden stand. Portraits of presidents adorned the walls: Washington, Jackson, and Jefferson. A cold chill surged through Katherine. Two additional spirits emerged, the original owners of the mansion. The first was an elderly man in a Confederate uniform. Possessing only one leg, he hobbled toward the room's double doors using a wooden crutch. Beside him appeared a husky black man wearing a red flannel shirt. At first, they were walking with their backs toward Katherine. But sensing her presence, they halted, glanced over, and scowled at her. The black man possessed large, blue eyes and wasn't much younger than the old soldier. Similar in some respects to fingerprints, their psychic energy left glimpses of themselves behind. These glimpses would prove invaluable.

Katherine drifted through more fog. Before long, she was in another bedroom, this one oddly shaped and containing a bed, nightstand, couch, and rocking chair. She could feel the presence of a new spirit almost immediately: a woman in her late thirties surrounded by a much more active fog. Gradually, the new ghost came into view. Dressed in a revealing negligee, she reclined on the bed. Through heavy mascara, her eyes scrutinized Katherine with all the intensity of a predator.

A destructive chemistry erupted between Katherine and the woman. The professor grew wary of her grin, so sardonic, twisted, and spiteful that it caused her to shudder. The woman's demeanor and psychic energy spoke volumes of nonsensical rubbish.

The only words Katherine could make out disturbed her deeply. "I know something you don't," the woman taunted. "Something you'll *never* find out." What followed was the woman's laughter. A laughter that was bitter and malicious. A laughter that was clearly an admonishment.

Interference, Katherine realized. *She's intentionally bombarding me with a screen of interference. She's hiding something.*

The woman vanished but her laughter lingered. As Katherine started returning to the world of the living, she felt a dreadful sensation, the same sensation she had felt just before she had encounter Sarah. There was something else lurking in this shadowy world, something well-hidden, refusing to be seen. It was a significant, powerful presence, and Katherine could feel its highly charged energy, a provocative energy laced with undeniable rage. The same energy that dominated the entire vicinity.

Without the slightest warning, the pain struck—a debilitating agony, as if a hammer had struck her forehead. The same type of pain Katherine often suffered after an exceedingly intense trance. This time it was much worse. This time she was in trouble.

***

Reaching into his shirt pocket, Jake removed two cigars and joined an exhausted Rick on the front-porch swing. He presented one of the cigars to his friend and confessed, "They're not Cuban, but they'll do."

Rick accepted the cigar with a bittersweet smile and a distant look in his eyes. Jake pulled out his lighter from a pants pocket and they lit up. Both men eased back onto the swing and gazed at the heavens. Thanks to the wind, the stars were out in full force. It was a clear night, but with the breeze filtering in through the pass, the temperature had chilled. The weather was definitely changing, Jake concluded, changing for the worst.

Trying to relax, Jake recalled what had happened when Katherine had come out of her trance. The only thing she managed to say was "migraine." Indeed, she seemed to be in dire pain. Lindsey had promptly whisked her off to one of the spare bedrooms. That was the last either Jake or Rick had seen of Katherine.

Consequently, they were left in the dark as to what had happened while she was in the trance. That was just over five hours ago. Now it was late, but everyone was just too keyed up to call it a night. Everyone, including Julian, had done their share to clean up the kitchen. The four of them had thrown a decent meal together: bacon cheeseburgers with a hearty side of Lindsey's homemade potato salad. Since every breakable kitchen item was now sitting outside in the trash can, they ate off paper plates.

After dinner Julian asked if Jake would let him use his computer. Apparently, something had gone wrong with his precious laptop. He wanted to "putz around" on the internet and see if he could find out some more information about the mansion. Taking him to his office, Jake set the kid up.

Intermittently checking on Katherine, Lindsey had settled down to a little television. So naturally, after a while, Jake and Rick found themselves on the front porch. This handy little spot with the incredible view of the pass had become Jake's personal sanctuary.

Contentedly puffing on his cigar, Jake came to an understanding with himself. Sure, he was feeling guilty about not being able to rescue Heidi from the swing. His inability to prevent Lindsey's savage attacks in the darkroom and kitchen only compounded matters. The fact that they were dealing with ghosts, spirits, or whatever they were, felt so *unnatural* that Jake had found himself wrestling with his own belief system. That, however, was no excuse to doubt Katherine Price. He'd already seen some pretty strange stuff lately, things he'd thought impossible. So why not cut the woman some slack? After all, she was just trying to help. Besides, due to her efforts, she was now laid up with one doozy of a headache. Jake had to admit that Professor Price had won him over, and, hopefully, by morning she would be back on her feet and able to communicate.

It was much harder for Jake to accept Rick's nephew, Julian. Between the kid's odd appearance and whiny voice, it felt like Jake's nerves were being melted into slush. Leaning forward, he finally asked Rick, "Your nephew, don't you think he's a little . . . weird?"

Puffing tentatively on his cigar, Rick nodded. "Don't get me started, Uncle Jake. And if you think he's weird, you should meet his father."

Jake rendered his friend a bemused smile. Thank God they were in agreement.

"Milo Humphrey's his name and he's an ex-hippy, a Timothy Leary-wannabe type of nerd." Rick chuckled. "He's got plenty of education, don't get me wrong. He was a professional student until my sister Tricia hooked up with him and started the guy on a normal path. But he's just plain weird. Not in a bookish sort of way like Julian but in a drug-induced kind of way." He sighed. "It's like all the drugs my brother-in-law took back in his younger days might had affected my nephew's genes."

Jake nodded. "You could be. Right now I feel anything's possible." Again he felt a smile cross his face as his mood lightened. "That reminds me of a joke."

Rick leaned back. "I could use a good laugh. Go for it."

"Why didn't the life guard rescue the hippy?"

Rick shrugged. "I don't know."

Jake took a hit from his cigar. "Because he was too far out, man."

Both men burst out laughing. They turned serious when the front door flew open and Lindsey stepped out, her eyes teeming with alarm.

"You'd better get in here, Jake," she blurted. "There's something going on with your computer."

Grounding out their cigars, the two men jumped to their feet and followed Lindsey into the house.

***

Rushing through the den's double doors, Jake could see Julian sitting in front of the computer screen. The kid's hair appeared more unruly than ever. As Jake, Lindsey, and Rick hurried over, to their amazement the room's lights kept turning on and off while a handful of words flashed across the screen.

At first Jake couldn't make it out, but as he approached, the message became clearer. "GET OUT!" it glimmered.

Then: "GET OUT OR DIE!"

It kept flashing the same two phrases, with the screen turning black in between. Sometimes the words were huge. Sometimes they were small. Sometimes they were in a white font, then in a black font. Except for the relentless ferocity, there was no noticeable pattern or rhythm.

Rising to his feet and backing away, Julian joined the others. Unsure of what to do, they huddled together. Jake was, perhaps, the most perplexed. Finally, he concluded that the computer screen was only a symptom, a visual cue of what was going on.

"GET OUT OR DIE!" it flashed.

Everything had gone horribly wrong, Jake realized. Completely berserk.

"GET OUT OR DIE!"

Jake's suspicions fell into place. Something hostile had taken over his computer and was transmitting threats to the screen. He considered turning it off but he didn't want to go anywhere near the keyboard or the power button, but perhaps he could pull the electric cord. Suddenly, Jake's suspicions tripled. Grabbing Lindsey by the arm, he shouted, "Everybody get down!"

The screen exploded, filling the room with projectiles: glass, plastic, and metal. Jake's computer screen had turned into a bomb.

Having hit the floor in time, both Jake and Lindsey heard dozens of fragments whizz by over their heads. To him it felt like Vietnam all over again.

As debris flew through the study, Jake turned and peered at both Rick and Julian. His friend had lunged behind the wingback chair. During the mayhem, however, something had struck his left temple. Julian had been slower to respond. With his eyes bulging and his mouth unhinged, he executed a bellyflop to the floor. As Jake watched, the kid cried out and flung his hand over the lens of his glasses.

The room grew quiet. Except for a pair of cables that dangled from the empty desk area, there was nothing left of the screen. Its debris covered the room and countless fragments had damaged the walls, left numerous cracks in the windows, and tore the hell out of the wingback chair.

Making sure Lindsey was unharmed, Jake rose and checked on Julian. Holding his glasses in his hands, the kid was shaken but okay. So great was the explosion that a metal fragment had penetrated into the thick right lens of his glasses. The kid was lucky he had such piss-poor vision; otherwise, he would have been minus an eye. Additionally, the bridge of Julian's nose was already appearing bruised.

Before Jake could reach him, Rick struggled to his feet. He was holding his left temple and there was a trickle of blood between his fingers.

"You okay?"

His friend managed a nod.

Jake shook his head. "Sorry, pal. I don't agree." He turned toward Lindsey. "Honey, would you—"

"I'll get the antiseptic," she cried. Avoiding the debris strewn across the floor, she rushed to the bathroom.

The One Who Hides

Clearing away debris from the wingback chair, Jake sat Rick down. He could see a small piece of glass in his friend's left temple. "Lindsey," he shouted over his shoulder. "Bring a pair of tweezers and a bandage."

Fortunately, the injury wasn't serious, as the glass had only lodged at the surface. Once again, Jake felt riddled with guilt. Any one of them could have been seriously hurt.

Lindsey returned with the tweezers, antiseptic, and a bandage. Kneeling down, she went to work, first removing the fragment, then cleaning the wound. "Sorry, Rick," she apologized. "This is the second time I've had to give you first aid in the last two days."

Trying to hold his head still, Rick smiled. "Yeah, but I'm not going to complain. It could have been worse. I'm just glad everyone's okay."

Julian watched Lindsey as she removed the glass. "I think I'm going to barf," he moaned, his face pale and distorted.

Jake whirled toward him, barely able to keep his emotions in check. "What happened here?"

"I don't know, Uncle Jake," Julian answered, shrugging his

shoulders. "I was just surfing around, trying to get more information on your mansion, when the computer went bananas. Almost like the internet had it in for me!"

"It's not the computer," announced Katherine.

Taken by surprise, the four of them peered at the doorway. Apparently, Katherine was planning to spend the night, as she was dressed in a nightgown and bathrobe. Grimly staring at them, she tightened the sash to the robe. Although she appeared healthier and stronger than before, she still looked tired and uncomfortable.

Motioning toward the destroyed computer screen, Katherine steadied herself. "This was caused by one of the entities. And it won't stop until it destroys you." As if in an afterthought, she peered at Jake. "We're in for a fight, and I have no idea of the outcome."

***

Easing herself onto the living room couch, Katherine accepted a half-filled brandy snifter from Lindsey. Swirling the contents, her mood had clearly grown pensive. "First of all," she announced, "there are *seven* strangers in this house." She spoke in the same, slow, clear, concise fashion as before.

Jake, Lindsey, and Rick exchanged perplexed glances.

"There are the six spirits that the three of you have seen, then there's the seventh, the one who *hides* and waits." Katherine took a sip from the snifter. Having just been removed from an unpacked box, it was one of the few breakable kitchen items that had survived.

Swirling her brandy, Katherine continued. "Actually, I'd like to tell you something about myself first." She hesitated, cleared her throat, and made eye contact with Rick. "I'm *not* crazy. I might be ill-tempered sometimes, and tend to involve myself with selfish, philandering men . . . but I'm *not* crazy."

Taking another sip of brandy, Katherine raised her legs onto the couch. "Six months ago, I became infuriated with the cheating bastard I was living with. In a rage of passion, I tried stabbing him and was charged with attempted murder. It was the lowest point of my life. The fact that I hear voices from the psychic world didn't help my situation. I was committed to Safe Haven until the charges were dropped. After that I stayed to work on my depression, something I've been ignoring for twenty years."

With doleful eloquence seeping from her eyes, Katherine sat back. "That's my confession, the short version, anyway. None of it means I'm insane. I thought you should know because your confidence may prove *crucial* in ridding this house of the seventh spirit . . . this *stranger* we know nothing about."

"What else can you tell us?" Lindsey asked, leaning forward. "Did you learn anything while you were in the trance?"

Katherine nodded. "Yes, not only have I learned a number of things from the trance, but from spending time in your house as well. The first ghost, the original owner, Colonel Breckinridge, resides in the realm of the *In-Between*, a world that exists between life and the afterlife. This world sometimes overlaps with ours. He's not happy about your presence here. As far as he's concerned, this is still *his* house and he would prefer to be living here alone. But the colonel and his friend, Jacob, have tolerated many owners through the years and would never do anything to harm you."

An attentive Jake ran a hand across his beard. "How do you know that?"

Katherine peered his way, took a heavy breath, and relinquished a morose smile. "When I encounter a spirt in *their* world, they leave glimpses in my memory. They're like fingerprints or DNA, traces of their history." She shrugged. "Call it a perk from being a psychic."

Satisfied, Jake nodded.

Swirling her brandy, Katherine took another sip. "Then there's the elderly woman."

Lindsey glanced at her husband. "Yes, we've both seen her."

"Her name's Abigail McClellan. She lived in this mansion by herself in the fifties and early sixties. She was born into a rich family and her inheritance from her parents supplemented her earnings from working as a file clerk in the San Bernadino School District. She never married and passed away in her sleep." Katherine frowned. "I think either she doesn't know she's dead or doesn't accept it. She means you no harm. I'm not entirely sure, but I believe she just might think *you're* ghosts."

Lindsey winked at Jake. "Maybe that's why she looks so frightened every time we see her."

"You know all this information from just seeing her in your trance?" inquired Rick.

Katherine regarded him intently. "Yes, absolutely. Her only concern is cleanliness. My other theory about her is that she's so compulsive that, rather than moving on to the afterlife, she has remained behind in the In-Between to make her former home a *cleaner* place. A bit obsessive, you could say."

"People can be so weird," cracked a bemused Julian. He sat on the floor with his legs crossed and his laptop sitting beside him. "Doesn't even know she's dead, and to top it off, she's a neat freak? How weird is that?"

"Then there's the mother and her daughter," Katherine said. "Sarah and Victoria. They both want to help you. Sarah possesses abilities that the others lack. These skills include the capability to communicate by moving objects."

"She also saved Heidi from suffocation," Lindsey added. "And another time by chasing off a rattlesnake."

Katherine again nodded. "Sarah's a *strong* presence but makes herself scarce. She and her husband, John, moved into this house around 1940. Her only child, Vicki, was born shortly thereafter. When the war broke out in '41, John enlisted and fought in Africa. He was killed in action at a place called Kasserine Pass during the Tunisian campaign."

Displaying his prominent overbite, Julian beamed a wily grin. "Yeah, I know that battle. We got our butts kicked."

"That's true," said Jake. "I teach high school history and I've done a lot of research on World War Two."

Katherine cleared her throat and continued. "In 1947, Sarah suffered another loss." She turned toward Lindsey. "While playing in the yard, her daughter Vicki was bitten by a rattlesnake."

Stunned, both Jake and Lindsey appeared to shrink.

"Because they lived so far from medical attention, Vicki died a few hours later. It was a loss Sarah never recovered from. She took her own life a few weeks later."

In addition to becoming more and more exhausted, Katherine was now quivering. "Sarah committed suicide upstairs in your bedroom. She killed herself by cutting her wrists with a razorblade."

"How horrible," Lindsey whispered. "I had no idea."

"There's another woman," Katherine stated, her voice growing weaker. "She's in her thirties, wears heavy makeup and a negligee. I gather this woman is rather promiscuous."

Jake glanced over at Rick, who seemed mesmerized by Katherine's every word.

"Although I've seen her, I can't tell you much about her. She's very secretive . . . and definitely hiding something. I think it's the identity of the seventh stranger. Perhaps if I found out more about her, I might discover just *who's* causing all these problems of yours." She cringed and rubbed her forehead with her free hand. "I'm certain she knew him, and they may have lived in this mansion together as lovers."

"Why do you call them strangers?" asked Lindsey.

Katherine flashed a bittersweet smile. "It's just a term I picked up."

Jake began fidgeting. "If you can't tell us any more about this seventh stranger, how do you know it's a man?"

Sitting back, Katherine could barely shake her head. Jake realized that she had pushed herself too hard. If she kept it up, she would be completely spent.

"I *feel* his presence . . . in your home and while I was in the trance. I can feel him right now in this room. He's *watching* you. I sense he was an evil person during his lifetime. And, in the spiritual world . . . he's much worse. He's *furious* about your presence here and wants you . . . obliterated." Setting the brandy glass on the coffee table, Katherine appeared to be drifting off.

"I think we'd better stop," Lindsey murmured.

"Maybe—" Katherine whispered as the four of them strained to hear her. "Maybe you've *threatened* him."

As Lindsey and Rick helped Katherine to her feet, Jake asked, "How could we have *possibly* threatened him?"

Again, Katherine shook her head. "I-I don't know. He doesn't want us to know."

Lindsey and Rick helped her up the stairs. Making sure the professor was comfortable, Lindsey put her to bed.

Knowing more about the "seven strangers" did little to calm Jake. Why did the seventh spirit want them *obliterated*? What had they done to threaten him? Most of all, what would he do next? The evening had left Jake more confused and frustrated than ever.

For the most part, Lindsey and Rick slept sporadically that night. Jake dozed on and off, which was some improvement. For the three of them, it was their first decent sleep for days. Both Katherine and Julian, however, proved the opposite. When sleep did come, it would be uneasy. For Julian, it would be both the most frightening and memorable night of his life.

Encounters

Julian dreamed he was downloading files containing pertinent information on the Breckinridge Mansion onto his laptop. Instead of a directory, there were dozens of ghosts haunting the screen. Initially, these ghosts were cartoonish in appearance, each of them wearing tattered bedsheets with punched-out eyeholes. After a few minutes, however, their faces morphed into jack-o'-lanterns, complete with candlelight flickering from their hollow eyes. These weren't ordinary jack-o'-lanterns but grotesquely disfigured ones, excreting black pus from multiple gouges and claw marks. They cavorted across the screen, plowing into each other continuously. *Gee,* thought Julian, *they're like the Keystone Cops. What site is this, anyway? Slapstick.com? Maybe the internet has become haunted. An asylum for slaphappy boogiemen.*

The screen went black, and Julian tried getting back onto the internet. When he was able to log back on, the librarian's heart nearly bolted from his chest.

Something had been waiting for him, something dark and sinister. This ghost was no funky bedsheet but a rotting corpse with hateful eyes bulging from their sockets. Suddenly, time had no relevance or meaning. They stared at each other for what seemed hours as Julian watched the putrid flesh seep down the face of what Professor Price had called the *seventh stranger*.

Without the slightest warning, the thing reached from the screen and grabbed Julian by the throat. It yanked him forward until they were nose to putrid nose. Its lips curled into a feral snarl. Its teeth were sullied and decayed. With rancid breath, it roared into Julian's face, "GET OUT, YOU FUCKING MAGGOT!"

The librarian sat petrified, his fear undermining his every thought. He could taste the stench of the specter's rotting flesh. Its enraged voice all but shattered his eardrums.

"LEAVE THIS PLACE OR I'LL GUT YOU ALIVE!"

What felt like a karate chop struck Julian between the eyes. He sprang up in bed wide awake, holding his chest, convinced his heart would burst. "Holy moly!" he hollered, wiping sweat from his brow. "What in bloody tarnation was that? A nightmare? A hallucination? I don't even take drugs!"

Caught in a whirlwind of turmoil, the librarian concluded that by the time he would be able to get back to sleep he would be eligible for social security. Unlike most people, Julian believed in ghosts. Believed in them *religiously.* In case the seventh stranger should pop up again, he decided to stay off the internet for a while.

Easing down, Julian nestled his head into the pillow. He closed his eyes, turned onto his side, and filled his lungs with surprisingly cold and musty air. *That's weird. It's summertime. Maybe Uncle Jake should cut down on the air conditioning.*

Julian didn't think his heart would ever be the same. Its thumping kept him on edge, but at least his breathing had simmered down. He needed to calm himself. As he dwelled on such never-failing diversions as algebra, statistics, and anthropology, the room grew even colder, sending an icy chill through him. He cringed, took a tentative breath, and—against his better judgment—opened his eyes.

A shadowy outline stood across the room. Julian squinted at the figure but was unable it make it out. Without his glasses, life was nothing more than indistinguishable blurs.

Sitting up, he reached for the nightstand. His normally dexterous fingers had become spastic puppets dangling on strings—puppets controlled by a sadist with a deranged sense of humor. *Geez, Louise. Where the heck are my glasses?*

As he searched, he kept an anxious vigilance over his shoulder. "Uncle Richard?" he croaked, his voice trembling. "Are you playing tricks on me?"

After a few near misses, Julian managed to find his glasses and slap them on. His stomach curled. He nearly lost control of his bladder. The person in the shadows wasn't his uncle but the most ravishing, sexy woman he could ever fantasize about. Leaning against a far wall, she smiled in a most provocative fashion. Her hair was long, dark, and wavy. Her eyes glowed through the darkness, the expression within them wild and lusty.

Oh m-my G-God! Julian's every thought sputtered into lunacy. *S-she's fondling her b-b-breasts! I-I need a flashlight.*

Dressed in a revealing black negligee, the woman casually loosened a single lace, further revealing her plunging neckline.

She's got the wrong room, the computer geek decided. *She's looking for Brad Pitt.*

With her open gown clinging to her pallid flesh, the woman advanced. The way she approached hadn't the slightest resemblance to reality. Gliding across the floor, halting, then gliding again, her eyes remained locked upon a paralyzed Julian. Her eyes then rolled up as she took to the air. Her arms raised, her fingers stretched, she floated toward the librarian until she straddled him. Although he had studied ghosts for his entire life, not once had he ever encountered one. They were most definitely invisible 99.99 percent of the time. Hence, as any gifted academic would assume, a living person couldn't touch or feel them. But to his escalating bewilderment, he could feel her body smothering him with her milky white flesh. It felt erotic and hideous at the same time but, more importantly, she felt authentic.

Suddenly, the woman's gown vanished. Seizing Julian by the wrists, she thrust his arms against the headboard. Never before had he felt so susceptible or been confined so thoroughly. *I'm the man,* he reminded himself. *I have the power to resist.*

Julian broke into a deluge of sweat. He could no longer distinguish the sex-crazed apparition through his steamed-up glasses. His ability to resist had derailed. If his calculations were correct, his virginity was about to come to a spectacular conclusion.

My God! I'm at the mercy of an Amazon.

Julian's pajamas were torn from his quivering body, the buttons circling through the room in a graceful ballet. Strains of *Boléro,* by the composer Maurice Ravel, echoed in the librarian's galvanized brain. A bizarre combination of fear and rapture overwhelmed the helpless nerd. "Oh God, what's going to become of me?" His cries were all but obliterated in the room's oppressive darkness.

"Oh, please, don't let this be a dream!" He felt enormous pressure on his wrists, throat, and what he referred to as his "long-neglected hard drive." Decadent pleasure rained upon him. A volcanic detonation began erupting. His glasses flew across the room. "And please . . . please let her be gentle!"

The encounter was not a dream—and the woman was anything but gentle.

***

Katherine Price was also dreaming. Her dreams, however, did not consist of computer ghosts or hedonistic spirits. For the most part, she endured the same dreams she'd been experiencing for decades. Except tonight, for some reason, her nightly journey ended quite differently.

Nine-year-old Katherine lay in a dark, dreary hospital. Her gown had grown damp with perspiration, her throat was parched, and a keen sense of loneliness ravaged her. Similar to a dormitory, she shared the children's ward with several other ill youngsters. Katherine had been stricken with the ear infection that had robbed her of her hearing. After rushing her to the emergency room the day before, her mother would never return. Helen Price was much too busy planning her husband's funeral.

The fact that his daughter had lost her hearing and his finances were rapidly crumbling proved too much for a sensitive man like Professor Lewis Price. Leaving no letter or warning, he took his life by throwing himself off a rooftop. His death brought such grief upon Katherine's mother that her mind snapped and she plunged into a bottomless depression. Before Katherine was discharged from the hospital, she was all but orphaned. Sadly, she would not discover the fate of her parents for weeks to come.

As she lay in her hospital bed, lonely and frightened, young Katherine looked to the other children. Every one of them had fallen asleep. She felt as if she were alone in that foreboding room. She hated the hospital, hated her illness, and wanted to go home. But most of all, she wanted to *hear*. Just a single word or the sound of the other children sleeping would have been enough. She was terrified that she would never hear again.

Then, much to her joy, Katherine spotted her father standing at the center of the room. Appearing as if he were a gift from a desperate dream, what stood out foremost was how tenderly he looked at her, as tenderly as he ever had.

Too weak to hold out her arms, Katherine called to him. It was discouraging not to be able to hear herself. She could only detect vibrations in her throat that was so harsh and dry she wondered if any sound had left her.

Standing at a distance, her father spoke. It seemed so strange that his lips remained motionless, but Katherine heard him perfectly despite her hearing loss. She realized many years later that she had heard him by means of telepathy.

Lewis Price told his daughter that they would never see each other again. He said for her not to grieve, that he would always be with her, both in her heart and in her mind. That he would guard her until she was fully grown. He told Katherine she would be well-cared for, and when she recovered from her illness, she would be left with an *extraordinary* gift.

Katherine asked her father if the gift was a doll or a stuffed animal. The college professor chuckled and said no, that her gift would be much more important than a toy. Very soon she would be able to see and hear people no one else could ever hope to. Most of the time, these people would be *strangers*, the majority good and caring individuals, and it would be *safe* for her to talk to them.

Fighting back tears, young Katherine said she didn't want to stay in the hospital. She told her father she wanted to go with him and begged him to take her. Lewis Price shook his head and stated that her time hadn't come yet, that she *had* to stay. He smiled and told Katherine he loved her. Then, within an instant, he was gone, never to return.

After she was discharged, Katherine lived with her maternal grandparents. Kind and loving people, they raised her well, sending her to special schools and encouraging her to attend college. Despite her hearing impairment, Katherine accomplished outstanding grades and, many years later, graduated from Sonoma State University.

Yet there were many things lacking in Katherine's life. Attending special schools while she was younger proved beneficial. The children there had their own particular needs and had much in common with her. Katherine got along well with these children and made friends easily.

The neighborhood children, however, were different. They were mean and caustic, frequently tormenting Katherine by calling her names that she read on their lips. Names like "dummy" and "deaf mute." Despite all the love and care of her grandparents, and all of her degrees and accomplishments, those horrible names left an indelible scar upon the soul of young Katherine.

For a while she was able to visit her mother. On Sundays, her grandparents took her to a "hospital" where her mother lived. This hospital consisted of several three-story, red brick buildings spread out over ten acres.

Katherine endured many strange and disturbing encounters there. Men and women alike stared into space, their eyes vacant and lifeless. One woman, dressed in a white gown and with gray hair that had been cut in varying lengths, followed them. With eyes that mirrored ceaseless confusion, she repeatedly called Katherine a name unknown to her.

"Psychic?" the woman slurred through her rotting teeth. "I know what you are. You're a seer, a . . . soothsayer, aren't ya? You can do all kinds of strange things, can't ya?" Then she would laugh wretchedly, a laugh that would lose control and deteriorate into hysteria. This happened several times, and the staff would have to drag the woman away.

Katherine hated everything about that hospital, even more than the hospital where she had lost her hearing.

Depending on Helen Price's mental state, some of their visits were better than others. On her more lucid days, she would recognize them and give her daughter a well-deserved hug. They were hugs Katherine would always remember: warm, caring, and comforting. Then came the questions. Was everyone all right? How was she doing in school? On other days, her mother would be curled in a fetal position, unable to acknowledge anyone. These catatonic states occurred more and more frequently as time wore on.

Helen Price's chronic depression deteriorated into a psychotic condition. She died shortly after Katherine's twelfth birthday. No one told the young child what her mother had died from. Months later, her grandparents claimed that it was grief that killed her, that she'd died from a broken heart. Much later, Katherine came to another conclusion. As far as she was concerned, her mother's death was just another form of suicide. Although slower and more painful, Helen Price's depression proved to be as fatal as a bullet.

When Katherine grew up, the men she dated were often cruel and selfish. They just wanted one thing from her: to take advantage. One relationship after another spiraled into chaos but Katherine persevered. Each time, she would pull herself out of an excruciating state of disappointment and continue onward. Focusing on helping those who depended on both her psychic abilities and her teaching skills, first in high school, then in college, she would battle the void created by the loss of her parents *and* the lack of a trustworthy soulmate.

While growing up, Katherine would hear both male and female voices—not by means of *audiological* hearing but by her highly receptive psychic abilities. Initially, these voices were distant and nearly inaudible. As time progressed, however, she was able to understand certain words and phrases. At first she thought these voices were signs that her hearing was returning. But her hopes were shattered when she learned about schizophrenia. The voices were not real, she learned, but rose from the depths of her troubled mind. Like her parents before her, young Katherine Price was teetering on the edge of sanity. It was only a few years later that she came to realize these voices were not of this world.

By her twelfth birthday, Katherine could walk into a room and know what had previously transpired there. She could tell by the mere touch of a hand what a person's accomplishments were and what would take place in their future. Occasionally, she was able to read an individual's mind. These abilities appeared to be centered around *emotions:* the stronger the person's emotion, the easier she was able to read them.

As Katherine approached her thirteenth birthday, she began experiencing visitations. People would appear from nowhere. Then, a few moments later, they would vanish. Sometimes these visitors were friendly, sometimes indifferent. Rarely were they hostile. Always transparent, they were just as surprised to see her as she was to see them. Since she didn't know who they were, she called them "strangers," the very term her father had used that night at the hospital.

It wasn't until Katherine was nearing adulthood that she understood who these individuals were. In that dark and dreary hospital room, Lewis Price had warned her that she would encounter "strangers" from beyond. For years, she considered her abilities a freak of nature. It isolated her and, as far as she was concerned, she was shunned by the entire world. She locked her secret deep within her subconsciousness. It was only after her twenty-first birthday that she accepted who she was. Whether

Katherine liked it or not, she had a gift, and as she grew older, she learned to control and understand it.

Normally at this point, Katherine's dream would detour to the lies and deceptions told by any one of her former boyfriends or ex-husband. How any man could be so stupid and arrogant as to cheat on a clairvoyant was beyond her. Yet they did, and she would always know. That was when all the pain, anguish, and sense of loss would come crashing back, sending her into an unforgiving and endless void. Then in her dream Katherine would be sitting in a chair facing a window. In her hand would be a knife, or a razor blade, or a scrap of aluminum. As she raised the object to slice her wrist, she would inadvertently escape her fate by plunging into consciousness.

Tonight was different. Tonight, her dreams manifested another ending. Sitting upright in bed, Katherine discovered a woman standing at the center of the room. Appearing to be in her twenties, she was dressed in a full-length white nightgown and her long blonde hair drifted around her as if being caressed by a breeze. Katherine recognized the woman: Sarah, the very person she'd encounter in her trance. Astonishingly beautiful and amazingly majestic, in many ways Sarah reminded Katherine of an angel.

When Katherine asked the nature of Sarah's appearance, she pointed at the window. Something was out there. Something she wanted her to see.

Then quite suddenly, Sarah disappeared. Katherine hurried to the window and peered at the front yard. Everything was cloaked in darkness except for the willow tree and the Sold sign. What was outside? What was Sarah trying to tell her? These questions plagued Katherine as she slept several more hours.

***

Katherine sat up in bed and clutched her throat. She'd grown parched and thirsty. She flung back the covers and gazed at the digital clock on the nightstand. It read: 3:11 a.m. When she was in her twenties and early thirties, she would sleep the entire night.

Since turning thirty-five, however, she would get up almost every night for a drink of water.

Stepping out of the bedroom, Katherine turned down the hallway. Darkness engulfed her. The wooden floor chilled her feet. The bathroom was between her bedroom and Rick's, on the other side of the staircase from the McKays' bedroom. Julian's room was located at the far end of the hallway.

Despite Katherine's efforts to be quiet, a floorboard squeaked. She stepped into the bathroom and discovered there was no need to turn on the lights—a nightlight lit the room adequately. She picked up a plastic cup and filled it. She took a sip and peered into the mirror. The room's dimness stripped away any traces of color. Her blonde hair had transformed to dark brown, and her green eyes had turned black. The details of her face were indistinct. Her long, white nightgown had changed into a dreary gray.

Katherine finished the water and returned the cup to the counter. Suddenly, an inexplicable chill passed through her. Holding her breath, she prepared herself. A malignant presence had just entered the room.

Taking an anxious breath, Katherine again peered into the mirror. Everything had changed. The room had disappeared. Fog had now taken complete control, swirling from the floor to the ceiling and shrouding every detail of her surroundings. The connection to the In-Between confirmed what she already had known: an evil presence was about to show itself.

The stranger advanced ever so slowly. What felt like fingertips inside her nightgown left a path of coldness across the flesh of her thighs to the curve of her breasts. The touch lingered for a moment then pulled away.

Katherine tried to turn but couldn't move. Somehow the stranger held her in place, his power gripping her in a web of his creation. She subdued her panic and focused on the mirror, watching, waiting, her heart pounding.

A pair of skeletal hands materialized from behind her waist. They ran along the length of her sides in a display of lust and domination, loitering briefly on her arms, then advancing to the nape of her neck. Never before had she encountered such audacity, such power.

Elongated fingers of rotting flesh wrapped themselves around Katherine's throat. It made no sense. From her experience, no spirit from the In-Between was capable of such formidable actions. This was no ghost. As she had suspected from the moment she had entered the mansion, something else was at work. Something demonic and evil.

A face emerged above her right shoulder: a dark skull with eyes clinging to their sockets. Eyes that were deranged, loathing, determined to extinguish her life.

Katherine tried to breathe but found herself unable to do so. The skin of her neck had become frozen. She still couldn't move and she had grown lightheaded. Her body felt as if it were encased in ice. A distant ringing signaled verbal contact. The seventh stranger was about to reveal his intentions.

Hello, Katherine, murmured a low, guttural voice. *Your helplessness . . . pleases me. There will be more pleasures waiting for you in my world. Pleasures that are cruel and painful. You will be my slave and I will do with you as I please.*

The grip tightened. Katherine's lungs agonized for air. She closed her eyes and, clenching her fists, challenged his power and audacity. She knew what to do and a way out. A method to break his grip.

You're not real, she proclaimed. *Your existence is meaningless. You can harm only the helpless and unknowing . . . but not me.* She felt the stranger's grip slacken, his power diminishing. *Be gone, you pathetic creature. I will vanquish you from the land of the living. . . and prevail over you.*

Katherine opened her eyes. All signs of the skull, skeletal hands, and the In-Between had disappeared. The grip upon her throat had ceased. Sweet, glorious air rushed into her lungs. Still, she had to brace herself against the counter as her lightheadedness dissipated. She put a hand on her chest. Her heart still raced, but gradually, it returned to normal. She stood motionless, catching her breath.

A moment passed. Her mind raced. A realization both profound and satisfying swept through her: she had just experienced a test of strength. A battle of wills. She'd won her first encounter with the seventh stranger. It wouldn't be her last.

The Spider

Lindsey was the first to wake. Seeing how bright it was in the bedroom, she glanced at her watch. Surprised, she decided she must have been exhausted, because she had slept until an unheard of nine o'clock.

Not wanting to wake Jake, she slipped into her robe and tiptoed out of the room. Making her way down the staircase and through both the living room and the dining room, she headed for the kitchen.

While passing through the dining room, she noticed the Scrabble pieces still scattered across the table. Once again, Katherine Price loomed in her mind. How could anyone not be impressed with her, if not fascinated? She had a certain charismatic aura about her, one that confirmed her abilities, paranormal *and* otherwise. A woman they had only met just yesterday but who had become their best chance to hold onto their dream home without being murdered. Perhaps their only chance. Hopefully, Katherine would be feeling better this morning. Migraines were no picnic and Lindsey felt a stinging tinge of guilt. All the woman was trying to do was to help them and, while doing so, had ended up debilitated.

Lindsey stepped through the swinging door and started a pot of coffee. Peering through the window while waiting for the coffee to brew, she discovered dark, hovering clouds. There would be no laundry-hanging today. She also looked at the swing set. Her heart sank. Feeling at a loss, she decided after breakfast she would give Heidi a call. She wanted to hear the sound of her daughter's sweet voice, tell her everything was all right, and that hopefully—as long as Katherine prevailed—she would be coming home soon.

Opening a cabinet door, Lindsey removed a small, green Tupperware bowl. Popping the lid, she retrieved two sugar packets. It was then that she heard a noise from the dining room. It sounded as if someone had bumped into the table, causing the Scrabble tiles to vibrate against the top.

"Jake?" she called over her shoulder. "Is that you?" A long, lingering moment passed. There was no answer.

Lindsey swallowed and recalled her childhood. Every time she watched a horror movie, when the heroine would investigate a noise, she would cover her eyes and holler, "Don't go in there, you idiot! You're gonna die!" The stakes were much higher than curiosity now, and even the slightest detail had become important. For the sake of everyone involved, she had to walk through the swinging door and see what was going on in the next room.

A vein on Lindsey's left temple pulsated. She dreaded what she might find, and she had a difficult time starting toward the swinging door. She'd already been hit on the jaw by a coffee mug, doused to the skin with chemicals containing acid, and nearly killed with an assortment of kitchen knives. She had no idea what else could happen, but she wasn't about to be a helpless bystander in her own home. Her parents had taught her well and drummed into her head, "Take the bull by the horns when necessary," not to mention, "Confront your fears and you will conquer them."

Straightening her shoulders, Lindsay inched forward, but then her legs stalled and her knees turned to what felt like jelly. Her parents had also taught her to, "Chose your battles wisely." Lindsey's heart skipped a beat. She almost never felt conflicted. *The hell with it.* Gritting her teeth and taking a determined breath, she crept toward the swinging door. Anxiety raced through her. Inching the door open, she peered at the dining room table, her eyes enormous. *What in Sam hell—?*

This wasn't a dream. Lindsey had known that from the start. She approached the table, leaned forward, and placed her hands on the edge. Her discovery not only surprised her but launched endless questions through her mind.

***

Five minutes later, Jake and Rick, both drowsy and hesitant, joined Lindsey in the dining room. Standing over the table, they gazed at the five tiles that had come together completely apart from the other ninety-five tiles. Lindsey insisted these particular tiles hadn't been touching when she had passed the table earlier.

Cleaning his glasses with his shirttail, Jake grumbled, "Ragno? What in blue blazes does *Ragno* mean? It's probably not even a word. Maybe one of the ghosts is some kind of con artist."

Rick frowned. "It sounds Italian. Kind of like *Ragu,* the brand of sauce I buy to make spaghetti with."

Lindsey turned to her husband. "Why don't you get the dictionary and look it up."

Putting his glasses back on, Jake departed, mumbling under his breath.

"You sure these tiles weren't like this before?" Rick asked.

Her eyes locked on the tiles, Lindsey folded her arms. If they started moving again, she was either going to wake Katherine or pay Heidi an impromptu visit. "Yes, absolutely. They weren't like that when I went into the kitchen."

Jake returned from his office, his Webster's paperback dictionary clutched in his hand. He flipped through the pages, murmuring, "Ragno, Ragno." Clearing his throat, he closed the paperback. "Nope. Nothing even close." He rolled his eyes, and tossed the book onto the table, narrowly missing the tiles.

"Lindsey, this is no help!"

"It's a clue," she responded. "A sign left by Sarah. I'm sure of it."

"I think she's right," Rick interjected. "We need to think about this."

Sighing, Jake flopped into the nearest chair and rubbed his temples. "So *what* in hell does Ragno mean?"

"Maybe it's someone's *name*, someone Italian," suggested Lindsey, glancing at Rick. "We've all been trying to find out the identity of the seventh stranger. And since Sarah and everyone else has been so threatened by this bastard, she decided to let us know on the sly, when the coast was clear."

The trio remained at the table, lost in silence, confused and frustrated as they pondered endless possibilities. They were so absorbed in their thoughts that they failed to hear Julian rushing down the staircase, louder than a herd of gazelles.

Nearly walking on air, and grinning from one ear to the other, the kid waltzed into the room, his face practically glowing. "Greetings, Earth people!" There was something exceedingly jovial about him, as if forty cups of Lindsey's strongest coffee had just kicked in. "You'll never guess what."

Staring at the tiles, his head propped in his hands, Jake murmured, "Hey, kid. Sure, I'll bite. What's new in La La Land?"

"Quite a bit! But I have to say, you're never going to believe me! Not in a million years."

"You've been nominated for the nerd of the year award?" Jake quipped.

"No! Not even close, but that would be interesting."

The kid's voice and enthusiasm were beginning to give Jake a headache.

"I know this is going to be hard to believe, but last night I experienced copulation with a nymphomaniac ghost."

Jake sat up. Both his and Rick's mouths dropped like blocks of concrete. Jake thought maybe he should check with his doctor about hearing aids.

"Yes, you heard right. I scored bigtime! I must say, there's nothing like getting ravaged by a kinky ghost. I highly recommend it. Furthermore, I rate the experience a ten-plus, or maybe even a twelve on the Richter Scale."

Lindsey covered her mouth, obviously stifling a laugh.

"If I'd known how perverse sex could be, I would have tried it a long time ago." Pausing, he tilted his head like an inquisitive puppy. "Do you think Professor Price would be offended if I asked her if ghosts have orgasms? I hope they do, because I wouldn't want to be selfish."

Jake, Lindsey, and Rick all exchanged bewildered expressions. It was already shaping up to be a bizarre day. And it wasn't even 10 a.m.

* * *

Sipping freshly brewed coffee in Styrofoam cups, Jake, Lindsey, and Rick listened to the graphic details of Julian's tryst.

"And then she was gone, completely vanished." The kid finished the rest of his tea and, slamming the cup down, wiped his chin. Turning to Lindsey, he added, "I'm sorry about the bedsheets. They should wash up okay."

Feeling nauseated, Jake shook his head. "That's disgusting."

Stunned, Julian straightened. "Why . . . thank you!"

Lindsey stood, staggered to the counter, and poured herself another cup of coffee. The stronger the better. "Is that the same spirit you encountered, Rick?"

"Has to be," he answered, his eyes still filled with amazement. "Can't be two like her. At least I hope not."

"I don't see how any of this is going to help," muttered Jake.

Frowning, Lindsey leaned against the counter. "Katherine said this woman is connected to the seventh stranger, that maybe they were living together."

Rick chuckled. "Well, she's not exactly *faithful*, is she?"

"Do you really think this Ragno's a person?" Jake asked.

Lindsey nodded. "Maybe we should check the internet."

Rick turned toward his nephew. "Get your laptop, Julian. See if you can find anyone named Ragno."

Julian rose to his feet, started to leave, then froze when he heard the name. His face turned white and his eyes rolled counter-clockwise in their sockets. "Ragno?"

Jake thought the wheels in the kids head were working themselves into overload.

"Ragno, geez, that sounds—"

"Julian, are you okay?" Lindsey asked.

The librarian turned toward Rick." I don't have to check the internet, Uncle Richard. I know what Ragno means."

Shocked, both Jake and Rick leaned forward. "Well, Julian," Rick murmured. "What are you waiting for? The suspense is going to kill us. What does Ragno mean?"

Adjusting his smudged glasses, Julian held his head high. "Ragno is Italian for spider, but it's also a nickname. Lots of gangsters had nicknames back in the old days, like Bugs, Bugsy, Scarface, and so on. Ragno Sorcha was a Chicago gangster who was active in the forties and early fifties. Not much is known about him. The mob moved him to Las Vegas sometime in the forties, probably to help Bugsy Siegel get the Flamingo Casino started. About four or five years later, Ragno disappeared. It's believed he was caught skimming money from the casinos, so maybe his bosses had him rubbed out." Julian frowned and bunched his frail shoulders. "That's about it, I'm afraid. No computer could tell us more."

Rick patted his nephew on the shoulder. "Nice work, Julian."

Grinning, the kid responded, "I know all about gangsters. They're radical, lawless rebels without morals. They've grown on me like a fungal infection."

"What about his first name?" Jake inquired.

Julian had to mull the question over for quite some time. "Marco," he answered. "That's it, Marco. He was known as Marco "the Spider" Sorcha, or among his Italian cohorts, as Marco *Ragno* Sorcha." He paused and scratched the side of his head. "Some names have origins and meanings that most people don't know about. For example, the name Marco is taken from the Roman god of war. And one of the meanings for Marco is "warlike," and better yet, "he who is at war."

Jake and Rick gazed at each other in stunned silence.

"Why was he called Spider?" Lindsey asked.

The kid leaned forward. "Well, I can only speculate, but Ragno was known to be a rather shifty hombre, even for a gangster. I think maybe the reason he was nicknamed Spider was because he spun an evil web throughout his career."

"Wow," murmured Rick. "You really do know your gangster."

"What about his mistress?" asked Jake. "The one that practically *raped* you in our spare bedroom. Do you know anything about her?"

Julian shook his head. "No, I'm sure there's nothing on the internet about her. Gosh, do you think I had sex with a gangster's moll?"

Rick nodded. "Kind of looks that way."

"Awesome," Julian shot back. "I can't wait to tell the guys at the Parcheesi club about this."

Jake sighed and glanced at his watch. "I still don't see how any of this is going to help."

"I disagree," said Lindsey. "We know the identity of the seventh stranger, someone Katherine *herself* couldn't identify. There's no doubt in my mind he's the one trying to kill us. The more we know about the guy, the more likely we can beat him. You have to admit, a gangster's a tough customer. It all seems to fit together pretty well."

Rick straightened. "You suppose this Ragno guy was a hitman or something?"

"Well, many gangsters were," Julian responded. "Any moron knows that."

Jake rolled his eyes and threw up his hands. "So you're saying we're up against the ghost of a professional killer? Now that's what I call a *shit* sandwich. Makes me feel a *whole* lot better."

"Katherine said he's *hiding* something." Lindsey peered at each of them. "And when I saw Sarah, she was pointing at the front yard."

"We know that," Jake answered, looking at his watch again.

"But there's nothing out there. You've been over that yard yourself, every square inch."

Discouraged, Lindsey sat back. "I know, but we're close. I can feel it."

"Well, maybe we'll find out more when Katherine wakes up," Jake concluded, standing. "In the meantime we're burning daylight. If you need me, I'll be installing a sprinkler system."

Rick stood and followed his friend. Just before stepping out the door, he turned. "Julian, you'd better steer clear of that woman. She's a bad influence. Maybe even dangerous." He paused and peered at Lindsey. "Would you let us know when Katherine's up?"

Lindsey nodded. "Sure. Don't work too hard out there."

Rick stepped into the back yard, leaving Lindsey and Julian to contemplate all that had been said.

***

Gradually, Katherine opened her eyes. She felt how she always felt the day after a migraine: groggy and exhausted. It took her some time just to get the bedroom into focus. Once she accomplished that, yesterday's events came crashing back, especially the one in the bathroom just after three in the morning. There was an evil presence in this house, and it wanted the McKays out . . . or it would murder them.

Sitting up, Katherine squinted at the window. Daylight was filtering through the sides of the blinds, but there wasn't all that much sun. Glancing at her watch, she discovered it was 4:30 in the afternoon.

Oh, no! I've slept over sixteen hours.

Katherine threw aside the covers and struggled from the bed. Lindsey had left a pair of slippers on the floor. Katherine liked her. She was a kind, considerate person and a strong woman, as well. Then there was Jake. Underneath a dozen layers of doom and gloom dwelled a *good* man. Hopefully, in a short while she would be able to solve their problem.

Putting on the slippers, Katherine made her way to the

mirror. Snatching a brush off the dresser, she began untangling her hair. Her reflection revealed a disaster. Her eyes were red and bloated, highlighted by deep, dark circles. Her facial color seemed a candidate for a mortician's pin-up. *What can you expect after sleeping for sixteen hours? Thank God the mirror didn't shatter.*

After using the hallway bathroom, Katherine returned to the bedroom and approached the window. The day was dreary and overcast. Deep within the mountain pass, ominous clouds were gathering. She didn't need to be clairvoyant to know a storm was making its way toward them. No doubt they would get some rain. Or then again, she ruminated playfully, perhaps the gloomy weather was an aberrant sign, a warning from the spirit world. A rare laugh escaped her. Fortunetellers had nothing on her.

She didn't know why, but she couldn't take her eyes from the old, weeping willow tree in front of the house near the street. How old could it be? They only lived to be about fifty, but in this case, Katherine suspected Colonel Breckinridge himself had planted it over a hundred years ago. Its appearance fascinated her. It resembled a man leaning over to the right as if in prayer. Surrounded by dead shrubs and rocky terrain, it was the only living vegetation for roughly 600 feet in front of the house.

Katherine spotted Jake and Rick over by the garage, standing on the gravel driveway. Rick must have been at the front of the property, probably by the Sold sign where he had left off yesterday, digging a narrow trench. He had removed his shirt, and he and Jake were taking a break from their work, drinking bottled water. From what she could see, they had been digging separate trenches toward each other. Her thoughts abruptly detoured. *And never shall the twain meet.* She groaned out loud. *Well, that came out of nowhere. Why am I quoting Kipling all of a sudden?* She shrugged. *Invisible things are the only realities.*

Sitting on the window chest, Katherine focused on Rick. His chest, arms, and shoulders were just muscular enough for her to take notice. His back glistened from a coat of perspiration. She recalled her vision the moment their hands had touched. It seemed inevitable; they would be lovers. His attraction to her was as intense as hers to him. Again, she didn't need her psychic abilities to know that. Yet their involvement wasn't meant to happen. It conflicted with a previous engagement—namely the scrap of aluminum in her purse. A person doesn't get romantically involved then commit suicide.

She grew disheartened. Life was full of risks. She had taken a huge one coming to the mansion, a dangerous place for the living. Being suicidal, she speculated, was to her advantage, as she had nothing to lose. Affairs of the heart—or in this case, falling in love—were extremely difficult for her. She had been wrong before and had suffered the consequences. Vowing to kill herself had put her in an awkward position. Love or death. It was either the scrape of aluminum or Rick.

Katherine stood, crossed her arms, and felt the beginnings of a delicate smile. The desire to give love one last try had indeed been growing.

She took a final look at Rick and returned to the mirror. She didn't want to be discovered spying on him. That would be humiliating. She had her share of issues, but spying on people wasn't one of them.

Later, she affirmed. She would help the McKays first, *then* make up her mind between remaining in this world or joining her parents.

***

The two men had returned to the trenches. Wiping his brow, Rick hunkered down and removed a rock the size of a softball. It was grueling, unforgiving work. The terrain was loaded with rocks of all shapes and sizes. According to Jake, this entire area had once been under water; hence, the river rock, both on top and beneath the ground. No small wonder his friend needed help.

Rick stopped to stretch his back and noticed they were losing daylight. Maybe it was just as well, considering how he felt. They'd been digging for some time now but, thanks to the terrain, hadn't gained much ground. Not only were they losing light, a storm was approaching. Dark cumulus clouds were coming straight for them. Plus, every now and then, lightning flashed. No doubt about it. One hell of a downpour was about to strike.

Good. We need rain. California always needs water. But then again, what was it going to do to their trenches? At least the wet ground would make digging easier.

Rick jammed his spade into the earth. It didn't go far. Once again, he stuck an object. *Wonderful, another frigging rock.* As he shoveled away the surrounding dirt, he struck it several more times. It didn't sound like a rock. It made a muffled noise at a completely different pitch.

The front door opened and both men turned. Lindsey stood on the porch. "Katherine's up and in the shower. Why don't you come in? We'll have dinner and then we'll meet."

At the very sound of Katherine's name, Rick heart skipped a beat. *Oh, brother, that's not a good sign.* He never had much luck with the fairer sex—a couple of failed romances through the years and that was all. Through high school and college, he attended various chess clubs, writing clubs, and took his studies seriously. He washed out at sports and didn't mingle much, so his social life never made it to the starting gate.

When he became an employed screenwriter twelve years ago, with deadlines hanging in the balance, he often locked himself in his computer room. Writing, he had learned over the years, was a lonely and solitary business. Although most woman found him attractive in an unmanly sort of way, his awkwardness held him back. Most the ladies who chased after him were flighty and unreliable. The few women he was attracted to wouldn't give him the time of day. He suspected they sought outgoing, athletic types, and wished them well.

He found Katherine different: a beauty with brains but, unfortunately, troubled. Every time he was in the same room with her, his body felt as if it were on fire. He didn't think it was just physical either. For some reason, he felt as if she were a part of him. That they were connected somehow.

Gazing at the approaching storm, Jake motioned at the garage just as a raindrop hit Rick's forearm. It was definitely time to quit.

Lindsey returned to the house and the two men lumbered toward the garage, their spades in tow. Rick forgot about the object he had struck. Although he dreaded their pending excursion into the supernatural, he was looking forward to dinner and a chance to get to know Katherine. He was curious, and hopefully, after tonight, his curiosity would be satisfied. Meeting Katherine as a patient in a private psychiatric facility wasn't a good start. Besides, she was a college professor and probably miles out of his league. But his gut feelings were pushing him in the other direction. Those same feelings were telling him he would know what to do after tonight.

***

From the front yard, something watched the two men. Its hatred festered. They were much too close. The time had come. As far as it was concerned, it had to be tonight. They would pay for this intrusion. They would pay with their lives.

Shattered Silence

Lindsey managed to throw together a tasty dinner of meatloaf, baked potatoes, and string beans. But no one seemed to notice. In anticipation of what was about to come, the five of them ate in conspicuous silence. Even Julian, forced to put aside his laptop, wasn't his chatty self.

Utilizing his computer, the young librarian had been trying to find any additional information regarding the gangster Marco Sorcha. As Julian suspected, there wasn't anything else relevant. The criminal remained shrewdly enigmatic, an untraceable rogue from a shadowy world, who, to evade the law, had kept his identity hidden. The librarian's research led into a blind alley: no known social security number, and no documented driver's license. If he had purchased the Breckinridge Mansion, he had done so under the names of Antonio and Doris Da Luca, who also proved untraceable. Even the man's death had been shrouded in mystery. Was he *actually* deceased? Most sources thought so, including the FBI, but no one knew for sure. The man had simply vanished. Marco Sorcha, Julian concluded, was a tough nut to crack.

It grew darker during their meal. Lindsey had to set her fork aside and flip on the dining room lights. It was only 5:30, but the storm had transformed the entire countryside into night. At six o'clock, a northerly wind rose, stirring Lindsey's windchimes on the front porch into a rather chaotic serenade.

Rick kept staring across the table at Katherine. Try as he may, he couldn't keep his eyes off her. She caught him a time or two, and embarrassed, he glanced away. She had obviously packed a change of clothes in her overnight bag, and she had gone from a skirt and satin blouse to jeans and a blue pullover. It didn't matter that she appeared pale and tired. He was well-aware of how migraines were a notorious ordeal. Yet, there she was, a woman beyond beauty. There was a certain profound intelligence behind her mysterious, dark-green eyes. Intelligence *and* elegance. Her face alone, with her high cheekbones and brooding lips, depicted an air of sophistication. As the evening progressed, Rick's attraction for her grew. College professor or not, he had made up his mind. When the crisis had been dealt with, he would act on his attraction and show her that all men weren't cold-blooded assholes.

After dinner, Jake, Lindsey, and Rick finished cleaning the kitchen. Before long they returned to the dining room table, each of them resolved and united in their pending challenge. Katherine had sorted through the Scrabble tiles, making sure the letters were facing up. When Julian finally closed his laptop, they were ready.

Shutting her eyes and placing both hands in front of her, Katherine called for Sarah to come forth three times, then she waited.

Rick heard the ticking of the nearby pendulum clock, the soothing rhythm of rain on the windows, and, depending on the wind's direction, the tinkling chorus of the windchimes. He glanced over at Jake, then at Lindsey. Transfixed, they were watching Katherine as if she were the only person in the room.

Again, the professor demanded, "I would like to speak to

Sarah. Are you near, Sarah?"

At that moment, all Rick could hear was the patter of rain.

Katherine repeated, "Sarah, are you there?"

Glancing down, Rick focused on the Scrabble tiles. Some of them began moving. Three, then five, then ten, then more. As if they were engaged in a massive exodus, they drifted forward through the remaining pieces, some going around, some pushing their way through. It was frightening how smoothly they traveled, as if each one of them were a living being. Other than the ghost of the black man who had shaken his fist at him, this was the most disturbing sight Rick had ever seen.

Gradually, the letters came together. Eighteen tiles formed five separate words. Together they read SARAH CAN NOT HEAR YOU.

All of a sudden, Rick couldn't detect the rain. It was as if every one of his senses were cemented to the tiles. Clearly surprised, Katherine took a jittery breath. It appeared to Rick that she was reluctant to ask anything further. But after a long silence, she straightened her shoulders and held her head high. "Why is that?" she whispered. "Why can't Sarah hear me?"

Twelve of the tiles inched away, leaving six. These six began rearranging themselves. Then eight additional letters separated themselves from the rest. Eventually, they joined the remaining six. The fourteen letters formed five new words, words that caused Rick's heartrate to double.

I WILL NOT LET HER, the message read.

The fairly neutral expression on Katherine's face vanished. In its place appeared an edginess. For an extremely intense moment, it was as if she had lost her ability to speak. She moved her lips but nothing came out. She cleared her throat, swallowed, and tried again. "W-who are you?" she demanded.

The letters slowly returned to the main cluster, except for three, the R, N, and O. Immediately, two other tiles came forward. The dining room lights flickered. Rick leaned forward, trying to see what they were. There was an A and a G. As the five letters joined, together they spelled RAGNO.

Gritting her teeth, Katherine snatched the tiles and raised them to eye level. She did this quickly, as if to trap whatever it was that had manipulated them. Clutching the pieces in the palm of her hand, her eyes closed and she slouched in her chair.

Jake, Lindsey, Rick, and Julian exchanged alarmed glances. They remained silent. *She's unconscious*, Rick decided. Once again, Katherine had gone into a trance. From the way she was writhing, everyone, *especially* her, was in for a horrific ride. Would she be okay? What would she find? Rick didn't know. All he knew was that he was worried about Katherine's safety, and all he could do was wait it out. He felt more than helpless. He felt useless. The prospect of sitting by, waiting for Katherine to come around, would be the hardest thing he would ever have to do.

***

For nearly a minute—but what seemed hours—Katherine was trapped in what appeared to be a full-blown nightmare. Around her was a swirling kaleidoscope, an endless tunnel brimming with flashing, red, blue, yellow, and green lights. The pulsating hues proved merciless. She had to look away or endure another migraine.

When she sensed the lights had ceased, Katherine opened her eyes and surveyed her surroundings. All she could see was the swirling fog. She was fully under, deep into a trance, somewhere unknown within the realm of the In-Between. Something felt different; other than that, she knew nothing. Not the time, the day, or location. That's how the trances were quite often. Hopefully, further along, things would fall into place.

After a while, Katherine was able to focus. Unlike her last trance, when she'd encountered the first six strangers, this time everything materialized in a slow, deliberate fashion. It wasn't twilight—a completely unexpected first—but nighttime or, possibly, the early morning hours. She was outdoors and the fog stubbornly followed her as she inched forward. She glanced at her chest and stomach then at her limbs. How different and disturbing. Once again there wasn't any color in the In-Between;

everything was muted in dreary shades of gray. The ground beneath her had grown precariously rocky and countless dried-up shrubs hampered her progress.

Gradually, Katherine's surroundings became brighter. Taking deep, steady breaths, she turned to her left. A pair of lights illuminated the immediate area. Several dark figures milled about, roughly seventy feet away. She crept toward the lights as quietly as she could. In most respects she was equivalent to a ghost in this world, and the chances of the occupants being able to see her were one in a hundred. However, they would be able to hear her if she stumbled or fell.

The illumination turned out to be a car's headlights. Two figures, a man and a woman, were kneeling on the ground. Despite the lights, Katherine wasn't able to see their faces, as all but one of the five figures had their backs to her. One detail, however, became disturbingly clear. The kneeling couple were in front of a pit and had their hands tied behind their backs. Katherine gasped. Traumatic occurrences that were extremely violent, often played out repeatedly in the world of the In-Between. What was happening at this very moment was one of those events.

Slowly, everything became clearer. Katherine could see three men wearing overcoats and fedora hats standing over the first two figures. From the way they were dressed, she suspected she was witnessing an incident from the early 1950s or late 1940s, an incident that had something to do with the man known as Sorcha and what he was hiding.

As Katherine's vision improved, she discovered they were beside a dirt road. The headlights were from a Plymouth sedan parked just forty-five feet away. Black, with old-fashioned running boards on the sides, the older model car appeared brand new.

The fog crept along the ground as if attempting to conceal the kneeling couple. Katherine pushed herself closer to see better. Although the three other men were dressed in heavy overcoats, the kneeling man wore only shoes, pants, a shirt, and a lightweight vest. The woman was barely dressed at all, just a black nightgown. She shivered between sobs that Katherine found heart-wrenching.

Much to her horror, she was able to perceive that one of the men was pointing a shotgun at the man on his knees. Another man leveled a large, shiny handgun directly at the back of the woman's head. A penetrating coldness swept through Katherine. The gravity of the situation had become all too clear. The couple were the captives of the three men, and the pit the man and woman were kneeling over was destined to be their grave. She was about to witness a gangland execution.

One of the men stood off to the left, facing the captives. Because his back was turned toward the headlights, Katherine couldn't see his face. He kept his left hand in his overcoat pocket and smoked a cigarette with his right. She sensed that this man was the leader, in charge of the two henchmen brandishing the weapons.

Taking a drag from the cigarette, the leader nodded to his cohort with the shotgun, who immediately swung the butt of the weapon around. In one quick, vicious swoop, it struck the kneeling man square across the jaw.

Katherine cringed, actually *feeling* the pain radiating from the captive. Now, suddenly, she became aware that he had already suffered hours of torture at the hands of the three men standing over him.

Although teetering at the pit's edge, the man managed to maintain his balance. The woman cried out and turned away. Katherine could also feel her terror. It was genuine, painful, and overwhelming.

Still casually smoking the cigarette, the leader leaned toward the kneeling male figure. "You better start talking. A lot of important people want to know what you did with the money." He paused and the night grew frigid. A coyote howled in the distance. "Did you launder it? Bury it? Or blow it on gambling and booze?"

The man on his knees lowered his head and began coughing. As he straightened, he turned toward the leader and spat twice, spraying both phlegm and blood on the man's chest.

Glancing down, the leader never missed a drag of his cigarette. "Defiant to the end, huh . . . Ragno?"

Katherine's entire body wrenched. The man on his knees was Sorcha, the seventh stranger, and she was about to witness his last moments.

The leader nodded to his crony with the handgun, who stepped away from the woman. Katherine tried looking away, but as in most trances, she was unable to do so. Pointing the weapon at the back of Ragno's head, the henchman cocked the hammer then paused.

Time slowed even further. A second felt like a minute. A minute, like an hour. It seemed as if a vacuum of silence had fallen upon them. Katherine's heart pounded in grim anticipation. Then a sharp burst of sound shattered the silence. Blood spurted through the air, followed by the woman's screams of terror. Sorcha's body teetered for an instant, then fell into the pit, followed by the sound of a lifeless thud.

Stepping forward, the man with the handgun fired twice more into the hole. The thug with the shotgun then straddled the opening and fired both barrels. Each time a shot was fired, Katherine's body convulsed. She didn't know why, but she often felt the pain of both strangers and victims in the In-Between.

The next sound was that of the leader chuckling. "So long, Ragno," he sneered, pitching what was left of his cigarette into the pit. "You got what you deserved."

Katherine could now perceive some details of the leader's face: dark eyes, hollow cheeks, prominent brow, and a twisted scowl. Turning toward the woman, he scrutinized her with a coldness that Katherine found petrifying.

"Well, Doris, that just leaves you."

Scarcely audible, the woman sobbed, "N-no, please . . . Marty. I don't know anything. I swear to God, I don't what Marco did with the money."

Katherine suppressed her revulsion and focused her entire attention on the conversation before her.

Again, the leader chuckled. "No, I don't suppose you do. But you've *seen* everything. Haven't you? You're a witness to our little get-together."

"Please, Marty. Don't!"

"I'll give you a choice," the leader offered. "You can join Ragno . . . or come with me." He paused and a devastating hush gripped the In-Between. "I think you know what that means." He stared her up and down, his eyes narrow and lustful. "You'll do everything I want, whenever I want, and you won't complain or have any say in the matter. Ragno said you were two bits above a whore, so it won't be something new to you." Glancing into the pit, he shrugged. "That way I can keep tabs on you. Make sure you don't talk to the wrong people." He snickered in a manner that was utterly venomous. "I'd say, considering everything, it's not a bad deal."

Nodding, Doris cried, "I-I'll go with you. I'll do anything you want."

Marty grinned and motioned to the others. They helped the woman to her feet and began untying her. When finished, they shoved her toward their leader.

"You always were a smart girl, Doris," Marty snarled from the side of his mouth. Then seizing her by the wrist, he rushed her to the car.

Katherine swallowed. This woman's relationship to Sorcha had now become crystal clear. As with many of her trances, a glimpse into the future made itself known. Doris would live six more years, miserable and guilt-ridden. Then, one night, she would slip away from Marty, drive out to the place where she had been with Sorcha, slit her wrists, and join those who resided in the mansion. Doris was the promiscuous stranger. The woman in the black negligee.

A flickering of light signaled the trance was ending. Watching the two henchmen shovel dirt into the pit, Katherine braced herself. Through a gap in the fog, she caught a brief glimpse of the immediate area. There was something just beyond the pit, something she hadn't noticed before.

Sensing its importance, Katherine rallied her psychic energy, but as always, it was almost impossible to stay in a trance once it played out. The best she could hope for was to stall for a moment. Straining, she locked onto the object. At first it appeared to be a skeletal claw, reaching through the clinging fog, intent on terrorizing her. Then it transformed before her eyes. It was a tree—a weeping willow tree that leaned sharply to the right.

Then it was gone. The trance was over. More lights—green, yellow, blue—flashed with agonizing velocity as if bound and determined to render her a migraine. Increasingly, Katherine felt herself slowly coming around, but in desperation, she tried to hurry the process. She knew the secret. She knew what the seventh stranger was hiding, and she had to inform the McKays before Sorcha did everything in his power to stop her.

***

Katherine gradually opened her eyes. Jake, Lindsey, and Rick were gathered around her, all three clearly concerned and anxious. A tentative grin crossed Lindsey's face as she offered Katherine a glass of water. Apparently, she'd been thrashing about so violently that they'd been holding her down.

"Are you okay?" Rick asked, his eyes brimming with apprehension.

Unable to speak just yet, she nodded. Her throat had grown parched and constricted. Although her forehead ached, she had avoided a migraine.

"Katherine?" Rick began. "Can you speak? Can you tell us what happened?"

As much as she tried, the professor was unable to verbalize. Talking was always difficult for her, and the dryness in her throat wasn't helping. Struggling just to raise a hand, she took the water from Lindsey, quenched herself, cleared her throat, and was finally able to speak. "Sorcha," she began. "His body's here. That's what he's hiding. He's buried outside. Between the Sold sign and the willow tree."

Julian rushed up, cradling his laptop. "Now I get it! He doesn't want you to find his remains because, if you *do*, it'll send him back to where he belongs. Shoveling coal at the bottom level of you know where."

As the librarian paused, an icy blast swept through the room. Before anyone could react, the kid's laptop ripped itself from his hands and soared through the room at breakneck speed. It spiraled upward and struck the ceiling, gashing a large hole in the plaster. Then it plunged to the floor, missing Jake by inches.

"Julian!" Rick hollered. "What's wrong with you?"

All color abandoned the kid's face. With perspiration dripping from his brow, he shook his head. "I-I didn't do that. I would never do that. C-computers are my *life*. There's something in here with us!"

Jake, Lindsey, Rick, and Julian huddled around Katherine. Jake peered toward the front of the dining room, his eyes bulging. Katherine stood and Rick pulled her into his arms.

On the wall nearest them stood an antique sideboard which Lindsey used as a china cabinet. Suddenly, its doors flung open with such force that it shattered both glass panels.

"Get down!" Jake screamed, taking Lindsey to the floor. Rick lowered Katherine and shielded her with his body. Julian ducked under the table.

A dinner plate shot at them from the sideboard. It shattered against the wall just behind Jake, showering them with fragments. Rick, Katherine, and Julian were bombarded as well. Plate after plate, saucer after saucer, flew from the cabinet at unbelievable speeds, only to shatter against the far wall.

When the sideboard's contents were exhausted, the antique began swaying back and forth. It toppled onto the dining room table, as the sound of splintering wood erupted through the room. Julian jumped away just in time. One after another, the pictures Jake had hung on the walls flew at them. One struck Rick on the back and another grazed Jake's forehead.

Then, quite abruptly, the room fell silent.

With his glasses knocked crooked, Julian squeaked, "Is it over?"

Trying to avoid the broken debris, Jake helped Lindsey to her feet. For the first time in their marriage, he saw tears flowing from his wife's eyes.

"Oh, damn it all! That was my grandmother's china. It's been in my family for *sixty* years." Sorrow etched on her face, she turned to her husband. "Someone could have been killed, Jake. We've got to stop this."

Rick assisted Katherine to her feet. His mind raced. He recalled how he had struck something with the spade that sounded peculiar while he was working on the trench. He was about to dig it out when they quit for the day. Stepping toward his longtime friend, he whispered, "Jake, I think I know where Ragno's buried."

Malignant Force

Gesturing toward Lindsey and Katherine, Jake told Julian, "Keep them in the dining room. Under no circumstances let them out." Turning to his old friend, he stated, "Come on, Uncle Rick. Let's finish this."

Jake felt as if his mind and body had come together for one purpose only. Rushing to the front door, he flipped on the porch light and flung open the door. Halting on the front steps, they both peered at the pouring rain. Jake didn't know if the downpour would help uncover the remains or if it would hinder their progress. All he cared about was finding what was left of Ragno and sending him to wherever he belonged. They had to act quickly—before anything else happened. Motioning toward the garage, Jake shouted, "Get the shovels, Rick. I'm heading to the trench. See what I can find."

His friend nodded. "Be careful, Uncle Jake. Don't take any chances." They separated.

Rushing from the porch, Jake felt the first of the rainfall. Sliding across what was now a thick layer of mud, he was forced to slow down. It was a large yard and he had considerable distance to cover. It seemed quite obvious now; the rain was going to hinder them.

The porch light illuminated the first thirty feet. Anything beyond that appeared indistinct, but Jake knew the yard held its share of hazards. Every now and then lightning flashed, followed by a roar of thunder. The lightning actually *helped* Jake find his way, and he used the dark outline of the willow tree as a guide. He kept scanning the area where Rick had stopped digging. It was near the front, to the left of the Sold sign and, of course, not far from the willow. He hesitated, then cursed under his breath. Not only was everything in front of him as dark as the Mariana Trench, but because of the downpour he could no longer see through his glasses.

Cursing some more, he shoved them into his shirt pocket. Now the yard was both dark *and* blurry, plus he had to keep wiping rain from his eyes. Fortunately, he could inch his way forward just fine. He shook his head. This was utter madness. It made little sense, but he trusted Katherine and now, surprisingly enough, Julian. Sorcha had been murdered and buried on their property. If he wanted to protect his family—and live anything similar to a *normal* life—it all came down to unearthing a gangster's remains. A gangster who in death, had managed to kick everyone's ass.

When Jake reached the area between the Sold sign and the willow tree, he hunkered down and waited for the next lightning flash. When it came, all he could see was the never-ending mud and the accumulating rain inside the trench. Sticking his right hand into the loose soil, he rummaged around. The mud oozed between his fingers as he probed deeper. There were numerous pebbles and, despite the rain, the contents remained surprisingly sandy. He touched an object not much larger than a softball but not hard enough to be a rock. He knew what it was and, adding his left hand, began wrestling it free.

Accompanied by an ear-piercing crack of thunder, a blinding flash of lightning struck the brush just across the highway from the willow. Turning toward the area, Jake was grabbed at the throat by an unseen force. What felt like a powerful *human hand*.

What in God's name?

Jake couldn't see his assailant but recalled the runaway swing and the invisible wall that blocked his attempt to rescue Heidi. There was no doubt it. Sorcha, aka the seventh stranger, intended to prevent him from uncovering what was left of his remains.

The malignant force lifted Jake high into the air. He tried latching onto his unseen assailant to relieve pressure on his throat. To his surprise, he discovered what felt like a pair of arms, undetectable but solid. The pain escalated. His windpipe throbbed. What he could perceive of his surroundings were rapidly disappearing. He was losing consciousness. He would be dead in a matter of moments.

The hell with this. I'm not *dying tonight.*

Mustering rage, determination, and strength, Jake brought his right arm straight up. Swinging in a perfect windmill-like motion against the unseen wrists—a maneuver he had learned many years before in boot camp—he broke the grip that held him. He dropped to the ground as wonderous air rushed into his lungs. His pain relented. Again, lightning flashed nearby. He wanted to get to his feet. He had to protect himself. But his bad knee kept undermining him. For the moment, he couldn't do anything but gasp for air and cough, leaving him defenseless.

The hidden entity grabbed Jake by the left arm and hurled him through the air. He landed on his right side, sliding along the ground. Mud splattered across his face and into his eyes. Unforgiving pain pulverized him.

Lightning struck, but Jake could no longer see the illumination. Forcing himself, he raised to his knees and wiped his eyes. Before he was able to recover, he was hauled to his feet and again thrown across the yard. He landed on his back, his right shoulder slamming into the Sold sign. Bone-wrenching pain erupted. Never before had he known such agony.

"You son of a bitch!" Jake uttered one obscenity after another. Still unable to see, he struggled to his feet. *God help me, how can I beat a ghost?*

There was no denying it. He had dislocated his right shoulder, rendering his dominant arm useless. He screamed in pain—then screamed again in anger. He'd dislocated his shoulder on the sign he'd repeatedly told their real estate agent to take down. He staggered toward the house. Fear gripped him, the same kind of fear he'd experienced during the course of one, long, unforgettable night in Vietnam.

For the briefest instant, long-repressed memories raged through him. The only other time he thought he was going to die had occurred in 'Nam, when their squad leader assigned Bill Graham and him to defend the southern slope of Hill 31, fifty clicks from Lam Som. They were ordered to hold out until dawn when reinforcements would arrive.

The Viet Cong waited until dark, a night very much like the one now, hampered by rain and lightning. Hidden in the brush they had rushed forward, for the most part totally unseen. Jake and Bill had fired their mounted M-60 machine gun. A grenade exploded at their left flank. Bullets whizzed above them. Jake took a slug to the knee, a wound that at the time he had to ignore. It was that very wound that now caused his chronic limp. But he and Bill held their ground for what seemed the entire night, but was probably about two hours. Just when their ammunition ran low, the Cong withdrew.

The next morning, they discovered the bodies of their foes that had been mutilated by the M-60. Nausea had ransacked Jake. Bill searched around and blew the brains out of a wounded survivor with his M-1911 pistol. Jake thought he would never be the same. During that unforgettable night, the same brand of fear that gripped him then—was now gripping him tonight. A fear that was both devastating and overwhelming. A kind of terror that made a person shudder and their guts turn inside out.

Jake raised his head and scanned the area between the sign and the willow. *I'm not giving up, damn it!*

He shook off his memories and overpowered his fear. Sorcha was defending the trench to the bitter end, so he was just going to have to find a way to bulldoze a path there. Short of dying, nothing would stop him.

From nowhere, a crushing blow walloped Jake across the chin. It felt as if he had just been hit by a block of concrete. It hit him again across the left side of the jaw, then on the right.

Battered, Jake collapsed beside the trench. He suspected Ragno had broken his jaw. Now, nearly past the point of feeling pain, a sullen laughter escaped him. The chances of success had been stacked against him right from the start. How do you fight something you can't see? How do you defend yourself against something that's already dead? These questions and more whirled through his mind. It was then that he felt the unseen hand once again clamping down on his throat, cutting off his breath.

As he was pushed into the mud, Jake realized his life was over. No matter how hard he fought, the hold on his throat was much too powerful. He'd been beaten. It was strangling him to extinction, crushing away his life. It was then that Rick screamed. Clinging onto life, Jake spotted the business end of a shovel slicing through the air.

"Let him go, you bastard!" his friend demanded. "Fight me, you piece of shit!"

Jake's throat was released, allowing lifesaving air to surge into his lungs. Gasping, he was thankful he was free, but now Sorcha was after Rick. He had to hurry, get to his feet, and help his friend.

Again, Rick screamed and swung the shovel at the enemy. Over the sound of the wind and rain, Jake heard Lindsey calling from the front porch. *Damn it, Julian! He screamed in his mind. You were supposed to keep her in the dining room.*

***

Lindsey, Katherine, and Julian stood on the front porch, horrified by the brutal events transpiring in the yard. Determined to help Rick and her husband, Lindsey turned toward the door, yelling over her shoulder, "I'm going to get something to help."

Lindsey rushed into the house and veered toward the fireplace, planning to seize the poker. As she approached, something moved on both sides of the hearth. Halting three feet short of the structure, she braced herself.

The gargoyle attached to the wall on the left side turned its head toward her, its stone-cold eyes fixed in a calculating expression. The gargoyle on the right side also turned toward her, its upper lip curling into a snarl. In perfect synchronization, they tore themselves from the walls, their eyes never wavering. Clouds of dust and rubble billowed through the room. Stepping away from the walls, they stretched their wings. As Lindsey watched in frozen uncertainty, they hunkered down into striking positions, their dark eyes morphing into blood-red.

Lindsey clenched her fist and eyed the poker hanging on the brass stand. She would never make it in time. The gargoyle on the left flapped its wings, a long string of drool trickling from its mouth, an ominous growl emerging from its throat. The gargoyle on the right licked its chops with a long, jagged tongue, its sharp teeth glistening in the dimly lit room.

They stood motionless. The grandfather clock in the entryway chimed, rendering Lindsey an unexpected chill. *Damn it, I have to get that poker. I just have to.*

Someone came up from behind and gripped Lindsey's forearm. A steadfast Katherine stood by her side, an expression of calm determination cemented on her face. "Don't be afraid. They're not real. Demand them to leave right now. And never to return."

Stunned, doubts sped through Lindsey. The creatures were standing not more than eight feet away, crouched and ready to pounce, each of them brandishing sharp claws, their lips drawn back to expose razor-sharp teeth. Could telling them to leave possibly work? It sounded ludicrous, much too simple, but . . .

Katherine tightened her grip on Lindsey's arm, her voice low and confident. "You have to believe what I'm saying. They're pawns, nothing more, summoned here to distract us. Dismiss them and you'll see."

***

Turning onto his right side, Jake watched as Rick was flung through the air, a hideous reminder of his own pain and helplessness. *Sorcha's going to kill him!* Jake had to fight off his pain and take action. With his anger spurring him on, he filled his lungs with air and rolled onto his belly. Forcing his legs to move forward, he crawled toward the trench. A stream of mud trickled into his mouth. His detached shoulder punished him every inch of the way.

Before he could get his hands back into the trench, Jake felt a kick to the left side of his ribcage. Excruciating pain ensued. Ragno had returned. Doubling over, he tried protecting himself, but the kicks persisted, each of them finding a vulnerable location: his ribs, groin, and even his bad knee.

The most godawful scream came from behind. The kicking halted. It was Julian screaming. The kid was charging through the mud, wind, and rain, armed with an indistinct object and waving it over his head. To Jake's amazement, the kid's weapon turned out to be his laptop.

"Die, you fiend from Hades," Julian hollered with shocking clarity. "Die a thousand deaths!"

Not wasting a moment, Jake crawled back to the trench. Reeling in pain, he reached in. He felt something round and solid. Thank God, the rain had loosened it. Gathering what was left of his strength, he began wiggling it from the ground.

Charging like a Green Beret in full battle mode, the screaming librarian reached the Sold sign. The wooden structure swung around as if on its own, caught the kid off guard, and struck him square in the chest. Julian's screaming was abruptly cutoff. He flew backward several yards. His precious laptop soared across the yard disappearing into the darkness.

Propped up on his elbow, Jake wrestled free what he'd been searching for. Immediately, the rain washed away enough mud to confirm its identity. Jake held a human skull that was battered, pitted, and cracked. He had no doubt it was Sorcha's. He could feel a bullet hole about an inch in diameter at the back. The skull was tangible evidence: Sorcha had been murdered and buried on their property. Because the terrain was so rocky, it was a shallow grave, roughly two feet beneath the surface.

Struggling to his knees, Jake held the skull high. "Sorcha," he screamed, lightning flashing all around. "Look what I got!"

Jake spotted a dark figure by the Sold sign. Hindered by the pouring rain, and lacking his glasses, he had difficulty making it out. Yet rain or no rain, glasses or no glasses, he knew it was "Ragno" Sorcha, the enigmatic gangster. Similar to the other spirits, the man was transparent and floating off the ground. Slowly, and quite deliberately, he turned toward Jake.

A deafening crack of thunder struck the ground thirty feet away, causing the earth to shudder and a column of smoke to rise. When it cleared, Jake spotted an open fissure, a reddish-orange glow radiating from it.

Barely able to walk, Rick joined Jake, grabbed his hand and helped him to his feet.

***

Lindsey stepped forward to the edge of hearth, glaring at the gargoyles. "You're not real. You're nothing but statues. You can't hurt anyone."

Both gargoyles reared back, their blood-red eyes squinting, their mouths grimacing.

Lindsey rushed forward, self-assurance pulsated through her. She snatched the poker from the stand and raised it above her head. "You're harmless frauds," she cried, her voice resonating through the room. "Go back to where you came from. Go back *now* or I'll *demolish* you."

The gargoyles shuddered, covered themselves with their wings and, as Lindsey and Katherine watched, vanished.

Then, a moment later, they reappeared in their original positions on the wall, a pair of statues and nothing more.

***

Glaring at the fissure, the lone figure remained stationary, his outline against the porch light menacing and surreal. Clutching the skull, Jake could only glare in return. Now that he'd uncovered Sorcha's remains, what ungodly atrocity was going to follow?

As if by means of a powerful vacuum, the figure known as Ragno was being suddenly swept into the rupture. Overjoyed, Jake tried to cheer but found himself too drained. Instead, he smiled and murmured, "Say hello to Hitler, scumbag!"

Sorcha fought the vacuum, first by sinking his feet into the muddy ground, then by struggling to reach the house. But the more he fought, the more the fissure drew him in, accelerating fiendishly, dragging his legs into the opening, then his body up to his waist.

Ragno fought relentlessly, as a continuous barrage of lightning illuminated the countryside, rendering night to near day. Jake managed to perceive the gangster's face, which was ordinary and unremarkable. With cheeks that were marginally hollow, he had no facial hair nor any distinguishing marks or scars. He possessed dark eyes and brown hair that receded on both sides. Indeed, it was the face of a typical forty-year-old man.

A moment later, Sorcha's features dissolved into rotting flesh. With his terror reaching an apex, his eyes glared festering hate. Fighting the turbulence, he screamed: "RETURN IT! RETURN IT NOW!"

Gazing at the skull, Jake understood. Ragno wanted his remains to be buried in order to continue his years of havoc: brutalities like throwing knives at innocent people or locking helpless children in refrigerators.

Jake glared at the gangster. Gritting his teeth, he replied, "Up yours, asshole." Straining his throat, he screamed and flung the skull against the willow tree. He threw it with every ounce of his remaining strength. The skull shattered into dozens of pieces on impact.

Sorcha relinquished a horrendous scream, one that sent Jake and Rick staggering. Once again the gangster's appearance transformed. Chunks of flesh sheared away. His eyes melted from their sockets. Bit by bit, Sorcha's features were sucked into the fissure until only a skeleton remained. The relic lingered briefly, battling the vacuum. Then, quite suddenly, it too was whisked into the rupture.

The rain and lightning slackened and Jake peered at the closing fissure. "Hope you enjoy the heat," he whispered.

Rick clutched his friend's left shoulder. "Good work, Jake. I'm proud of you. You just defeated something more than a ghost. Something more like a demon."

A proud and beaming Lindsey rushed over. Tossing the poker to the ground, she put her arms around her husband, kissed him, then held him tightly. "Are you okay?"

Jake winced and she loosened her embrace. He managed a frail smile and nodded. "I'm in excellent shape except for a dislocated shoulder and a near broken jaw, not to mention my pulverized body." He chuckled and thought the gesture would put him in the hospital. "Nothing that a year of healing can't cure."

"We'll take care of those injuries," replied Lindsey. "I've relocated shoulders at least a dozen times."

Katherine hurried toward Rick and ran her hands over his chest and arms, her concern obvious in her eyes even in the dim light. "Are you hurt?"

He took her by the hand. "I've had better days, but I'm all right," he assured her.

The professor smiled, caressed his cheek, and kissed him on the lips.

Observing the couple with keen interest, Jake turned to Lindsey. "Trust me, they're going to be an item." He took a much needed breath and motioned at what Lindsey had dropped on the ground. "You brought the poker?"

Before his wife could answer, a distant moan sounded. Jake's heart nearly stopped. "Now what?"

Still moaning and caked in mud, an unrecognizable Julian struggled to a sitting position. In all the excitement, Jake had forgotten about him. Along with Lindsey, he rushed over and helped the librarian to his feet.

"Am I dead, Uncle Jake?"

It was strange, but now, suddenly, he didn't mind Julian calling him uncle. "No, you're going to be all right. Thanks to you, Katherine, and Rick, we're all going to be great."

"You mean I did good?"

Jake held him by the shoulders. "You were *terrific,* Julian. You saved my life, and your uncle's, too. We owe you big time."

Gloating with pride, the librarian whimpered, "Good grief. That's absolutely groovy."

Stepping up to his nephew, Rick handed him the laptop and his glasses. In battered condition and covered in mud, both the computer and the glasses were undoubtedly beyond repair. "Honestly, Julian," his uncle sighed. "What were you going to do with your laptop? Delete the boogeyman?"

The librarian cracked a lopsided grin. "I don't know, Uncle Richard. It was all I had."

Smiling, Jake turned toward Lindsey. It felt good to smile again. Despite his injuries, he hadn't felt this good since moving into the mansion. "You know, honey," he murmured, "I think it's time we finished unpacking."

With that the five of them made their way into the house.

***

Jake, Lindsey, and Julian had gone to bed and Rick and Katherine had settled into the living room couch. The grandfather clock in the entryway chimed 2 a.m. The storm outside had lifted. Normally, Katherine would be exhausted, especially considering all that had happened. But not tonight. Tonight, she had helped banish a malignant force that wanted the McKays dead. The five of them had sent a formidable evil from the In-Between to its permanent residence in the hereafter.

"I don't get it," Rick murmured. He was lying on the couch, his head on Katherine's lap. "How could a ghost become some type of vicious demon? I thought that only happened in the movies."

Katherine ran her fingers through his hair. Her heart swelled. Rick was a good man. Someone she wished she had met ten years ago. Not only was she attracted to him, she respected him, a good foundation for a relationship. "He was a *demonic* spirit," she said softly, gazing at the fireplace where the gargoyles used to be. Shortly after they had finished with Sorcha, Jake had taken his sledgehammer out of the garage and put it to work. Now the creatures were nothing but harmless debris.

"I'm sure Sorcha had an obsession with the occult during his lifetime," she murmured with a smile. "And he must have participated in at least one satanic ritual." She ran her fingertips across Rick's cheek. "There was definitely some type of diabolical contact made *before* he was murdered that created a pact. Some people call it selling your soul. It's rare but it's happened before. Years ago in Wisconsin, an avenging entity turned demonic and murdered several people over a span of more than thirty years. It took a psychic to put a stop to it."

Rick gazed up, his eyes not only taking her in but reflecting his misgivings. "Ghosts, demons, spirits, it's all too much. I wish I had never heard of them. People are going to think we're insane. I could make tons of money by writing a screenplay about this crazy disaster because moviegoers *love* that kind of stuff." He sighed and shook his head. "But one time around is more than enough. I don't want to relive it. I'm going to do my best to forget the whole mess."

Katherine nudged him toward her. "You'll change your mind, I guarantee it."

They both laughed.

Katherine peered into his eyes. "And as far as ghosts are concerned, you'd better brace yourself, because I think you're going to learn a lot more about the spirit world hanging around with a clairvoyant." She pulled him up until they were face to face. "Now relax and kiss me."

Aftermath

After Lindsey and Rick hugged Julian goodbye, the librarian extended his hand toward Jake. With his right arm in a sling, Jake took the kid's hand, then added a hug of his own. "Come back any time, kiddo. I mean it. You may look and act like a timid computer nerd, but you're a bona-fide Audie Murphy, medals and all."

Grinning in record-breaking fashion, Julian gushed, "In that case, I'll see you next week."

Jake's face turned pale. He stood speechless and wide-eyed.

The librarian sniggered and added, "I'm kidding, Uncle Jake. Honest, just kidding."

Julian turned and opened the door to his Volvo. Katherine approached, hugged him goodbye, and whispered in his ear. The kid's reaction caught Jake off guard. His eyes bulged and his face turned a ghastly shade of gray. Without another word, he jumped into his vehicle, started the engine, and roared out of the driveway.

After watching the Volvo race toward the interstate, Rick turned and asked, "What did you tell him, Katherine? He looked like something just crept over his grave."

A tenuous smile crossed her face. "I told him to get medical attention."

"Medical attention? What for?"

Katherine sighed. "Remember the woman in the black negligee?"

Rick's eyes all but popped out. "Of course. Who could forget her?"

"She had syphilis when she killed herself."

Stunned, Rick shook his head. "Don't ever sleep with a promiscuous ghost," he murmured. "Any moron knows that."

***

Jake and Lindsey were on the verge of tears as they made their way to Rick's Chrysler. After hugging Katherine goodbye, Lindsey eased the passenger door shut. "You *literally* saved our lives," she said. "Thank you for everything. You took a dangerous chance for people you didn't even know. Please come back again soon. We'd love to see you."

Glancing over at Rick, who was saying farewell to Jake, Katherine blushed and nodded. "I'll come back. I'm sure Rick will insist."

On the other side of the Chrysler, Jake murmured, "Well, I guess you've had one hell of a vacation, huh, Uncle Rick?"

"It's been quite a ride," his friend agreed. "Makes me wonder what you've got in store for us next time."

Jake chuckled and, glancing at Katherine, flashed a knowing grin. "I'm glad you're taking her home, Kemosabe. I'm hoping for the best for you two, if you get my drift."

Opening his car door, Rick appeared smitten. "I still have a few more days of vacation before I start my next project. Maybe, if I play my cards right, I won't have to spend them alone."

The two friends shook hands then embraced.

"Don't be a stranger," Jake said.

Both of them burst out laughing. Rick had to clear his throat. "Stranger, huh? Was that a Freudian slip or a pun?"

Jake shrugged. "Completely accidental." He adjusted his glasses and placed his hands on his hips. "Looks like the term *stranger* has taken on new meaning."

***

As Jake and Lindsey watched, Rick backed out of the driveway and, turning south, pulled onto the road. Waving through the open window, he sped away.

Sitting beside Rick in the front seat, Katherine reached into her purse. Cautious not to let him see, she removed the scrap of aluminum and held it in the palm of her hand. She studied it intently, examining its sharpness. Taking a deep breath, she put her hand out through the window and allowed the wind to whisk the small piece of metal away.

Rick leaned toward her and she kissed him on the cheek. Katherine beamed. A sense of joy surged through her. This time she knew. Deep in her heart, and even deeper into her never-stronger psychic abilities, she knew without a doubt. Her years of grief were over. All her tomorrows would be brighter, filled with a happiness she had never known.

***

Walking arm in arm with her husband, Lindsey announced, "I'll drive down to my sister's this afternoon. It's time for Heidi to come home."

Jake nodded. "That sounds great to me, Lindsey. I'll go with you."

Peering at their house, Jake felt both relief and gratification. Heidi was returning to a safe and secure environment. Although there were six spirits still inhabiting their mansion, as long as they behaved themselves, he could care less. Not many folks could say they shared their home with a half dozen ghosts, and that made Jake feel special. Now if he could only figure a way to get those so-called strangers to pay rent . . .

***

As Jake and Lindsey returned to their home, a clandestine presence watched them from an upstairs window. Doris wasn't happy. Not in the least.

First these intruders had banished the only person she'd ever loved, and now, thanks to them, she was without his companionship. How dare they! Marco was a lot of things, including a criminal, and a malicious spirit, but he was most often good to her, and he was all she had. The situation had grown intolerable. Anger and frustration consumed her. She would have to take action. Do something extremely *intense.* Something *vengeful.* Something that would render a distinct and painful message.

Six months later

After completing the tour of the Breckinridge Mansion, Mrs. Hampton turned toward the young couple, Mary and Tom Davidson. They stood before the fireplace, the walls on both sides having been repaired and freshly painted. The sparkle that had previously brightened the real estate agent's eyes had long since disappeared.

"I want to be *perfectly* honest with you. There are always a few problems with a house this old." Resisting the urge to wring her hands, Mrs. Hampton continued. "Just a few annoying little problems that Jake and Lindsey McKay discovered could drive a person away." She relinquished a faint chuckle and fanned her face with her hand. "Unfortunately, even drive them out of California." She shook her head. "Some people just aren't cut out for an occasional bump or a few creaks every now and then."

Tom glanced at Mary and she eagerly nodded. "This place is *gorgeous,* and we love it. I don't care if it's haunted. We'll work it out. When can we move in?"

A rather nervous Mrs. Hampton turned toward the living room window. To her disbelief—and for the first time ever—she spotted one of the ghosts, a transparent, elderly Confederate soldier. Hobbling about on a wooden crutch between the For Sale sign and the weeping willow tree, the gentleman was dressed in full military regalia.

"Mrs. Hampton?" probed Tom.

Colonel Breckinridge suddenly halted. Amazingly enough, he appeared to be sensing that someone was watching him. Taking his time, he turned around.

"Mrs. Hampton?"

Grinning as if he had just singlehandedly won the Civil War, the colonel raised his right hand while staring at the real estate woman. She thought he was going to wave, or salute, but to her indignation, he extended his middle finger.

"Mrs. Hampton!" hollered Tom. "When can we move in?"

With the corners of her mouth twitching, the real estate agent turned toward the couple. "Move in?" she muttered, her eyes raised and glazed over as if she were talking to something floating over their heads. "You can move in as soon as we can get this place exterminated."

Author's Notes

Back in the 1990s, I wrote "The Seventh Stranger" as a short story on a minor-league word processing program. It was a lengthy story, almost but not quite a novella, one of seven stories intended for my unpublished anthology, *Mayhem*. Thank God I had the foresight to print out copies—which found their way to the very back of my file cabinet—because, twenty years later, when I dug out those stories with the intention of publishing them, the word processing program I saved them on couldn't be read by Microsoft Word.

Almost all the stories were enjoyable and more than worthy to be resurrected. Starting with "Detour," I typed page after page into Word—a true labor of love—giving each story a complete overhaul. All but one of these stories have since been published, including *Stalkers*, (my second horror novel), "The Wreck of the Lady Lydia," "Birds of a Feather," and "The Cellar," included in my anthology *Shadowland,* and the aforementioned "Detour," which is featured in my earlier anthology, *Shreds*.

With "The Seventh Stranger," I decided to try scanning the material into Word. I had attempted this before with disastrous results, much of the material being mutilated beyond recognition.

Evidently, Word had improved over the years; the results this time around were much better. Once the scanning was accomplished, I completed a more-than-year-long edit. Since the story's length fell short of a novel, I added new scenes, fleshed out the characters, and inserted a few additional characters. I'm happy with the results and delighted to have finally published *The Seventh Stranger* after twenty-eight years of hibernation.

—Michael Raff, May, 2023

About the Author

Michael Raff fell in love with writing at the age of thirteen while living in Chicago. He attended creative writing courses at Cypress College. After publishing his romantic memoir, *Special,* he completed four horror anthologies—*Seven: Tales of Terror, Scare Tactics, Shreds*, and *Shadowland*—and his non-horror anthology, *Something Different,* which features several award-winning stories. He has also written three horror novels: *Skeleton Man, Stalkers,* and this latest one, *The Seventh Stranger.*

Michael co-founded Nevermore Enterprises with fellow author Roberta Smith to promote their books and activities and he has remained active in the High Desert Branch of the California Writers Club (HDCWC) since 2011, frequently serving on their board. He has published three stories in the California Writers Club's statewide magazine, *The Literary Review*, two stories in online magazines, and several in a number of HDCWC anthologies.

He is the author of numerous short stories, several of them award winning, including "The Salvation of Edward Wilson," and "Donnie Sharp," which took first place in the HDCWC's acclaimed anthology, *Unforgettable.* His horror stories "Tell Me A Story" and "Bed Thirteen" have been published in the Dragon Soul Press's anthologies *Haunt* and *Beautiful Darkness.*

He lives in Hesperia, California, with his wife, Joyce, and a variety of dogs, cats, goats, and a horse named Freckles. For more information, visit his website at mraffbooks.com.

Printed in Great Britain
by Amazon

26560989R10126